FLAME

Smoke and Moonlight: Book 2

By

A.M. Burns

See what A.M. Burns is up to.
Visit his website www.amburns.com
Sign up for his email list

Copyright 2020 © MysticHawker Press

http://www.mystichawker.com/

ISBN: 978-1-945632-92-1

Edited by Robert Brownson
Cover art by Silver Circle Images

Other Books by A.M. Burns

Shifter Force
1: Visions of Rage
2: Visions of Shadows
3: Visions of Stars

Yellow Sky Coven:
1: Blood Moon Yellow Sky
2: Dark Stars of Dallas

Stand Alone Books:
The Black Fin Case

YA Books:
Coyote's Pup

Familiar Series:
1: Familiar Path
2: Familiar Spirit

Books in the Infragilis Universe.

Smoke and Moonlight
1:Spark

Solstice Properties Mysteries
1: Second Story Hex
2: Watchtower WooWoo
3: Mid-Century Monster

Tempest Academy Prologue
Running in a Pack
Into the Sky
Shifting Tides

1

The warm water was a feature of the house I didn't think I'd ever stop appreciating. After years of patrols and temporary quarters wherever the US Army sent my unit of Rangers, having a permanent base of operations with hot and cold running water wasn't going to get old any time soon. It had taken some searching and trusting in new friends before I found a soap I could handle the scent of. The wolf that amplified my senses didn't like any mass-produced soaps and shampoos. They were too strong-smelling. I was constantly wondering how I'd lived over thirty years and not realized how nasty a lot of them were. But having witches and mages for friends, as well as being guardian to a Djinn girl, was being a real eye-opener.

A softly-scented shampoo I used didn't lather as much as the commercial stuff did, but it still got my short silver hair squeaky clean, and that was what was important. No more sand down to my scalp that took half an hour to work clean.

With fainter scents flowing around the bathroom, it was still enough to dull my sensitive nose. The bacon cooking in the kitchen was strong, but something had changed. There was another in the house. Garnet Godfree wasn't due to be over for another half an hour, and she wasn't normally early. Someone had entered my domain and was in the kitchen with Vash, my Djinn ward.

I slammed the water off, not bothering to get the rest of the shampoo out of my hair. Grabbing a towel to wrap around my waist I rushed down the hall and into the kitchen. I should've stopped and grabbed my magical pistol Stormbringer off the hook near my bedroom door, but I'd make do with my fist and, if need be, my claws. As an ex-Ranger, and a werewolf, I was my own weapon.

My feet were still slightly wet and slipped on the smooth tile floor as I rushed into the kitchen. I slid and would've gone down if I hadn't been able to catch myself on the counter.

Gavin Harris, mage and good friend, stood a few feet away, looking at the meal Vash was preparing at the stove.

Vash, floated just high enough to see what she was doing. An almost constant rain of golden sparks cascaded from her long red hair to fade away before they hit the white tile floor below her. Since she had discovered cooking, it had become one of her favorite things to do.

"Lucas, you're making me feel overdressed." Harris grinned but didn't laugh.

Heat washed through my cheeks as stupid rushed through my brain. Where Garnet wasn't prone to being early, and often not even on time, Harris was. But Harris wasn't supposed to be over. The bacon was mingling with his basic woody smell. Applewood and pine mingled and distorted the scent I should've recognized. "Sorry." I ran my hand through my still soapy hair. "Caught a weird scent and came running."

Harris waved me out of the kitchen. "It's just me. Go rinse off."

Vash giggled. The sound was somewhere between a bird twittering and bells ringing.

Without another word, I turned and retreated down the hall. Even after several months of trying to totally understand what I had gone through after the werewolf attack had killed part of my unit, followed by the Effrit attack that finished them off, I still didn't have everything under control. Between PTSD and being a werewolf, I was more lost than I was home.

After a quick rinse, I pulled on jeans and a Polo shirt that wasn't overly tight across my chest. I swore I was growing more muscular with each full moon. It wasn't much longer before I made it back to the kitchen.

With a dishtowel over his arm, Harris pointed me toward the table where three plates waited. "I hope it's okay, Vash insisted even though I had breakfast before heading over."

"Sure." I glanced at the clock. If I was going to make my first stop, I was going to need to get moving soon. "Can't take too long. Are you covering for Garnet?"

"Yeah." Harris set the plate of bacon on the table as Vash brought over a stack of pancakes. "Garnet got called in to substitute teach an art class today. She would've come by and gotten Vash, but she had to be there a couple of hours ago, and she wouldn't have been able to meet up with you after your group session."

"So, Gavin's going to sit with me." Vash gestured toward the fridge and as more magical sparks fell from her long red hair, it opened. The bottle of syrup and tub of margarine floated to the table. "I told him that was okay."

"It is." I caught the butter before it landed. Vash and I had had a long discussion about when it was okay to use magic around the house and when it wasn't. Since we were a decent distance from the neighbors, and unless they were using military-grade equipment, they wouldn't be able to see into the house, it depended on who was over. Most of our non-neighbor friends were magical in some way, so it was safe. The thing was, it still hit me as weird to have things like condiments floating around the room. I was adjusting. "Thanks, Harris. I appreciate the help."

Harris snagged a couple of pancakes and put them on his plate. "No worries. I didn't really have anything pressing planned. Thought I might drive out and check some of the local wards I keep up to let me know who comes and goes in my territory." He grinned. "I'm just glad I don't' have to go around peeing on things to mark my territory."

I shook my head. "And I don't want to be an alpha, so I don't plan on doing that either." The fact that I couldn't be around howling wolves without my PTSD flaring up, made it a sure thing that I was going to be a mostly lone wolf, other than my wolf-life coach, Chad Kilkari, who knew not to howl around me. We got together with non-wolves in the area during the full moon and they helped me get to know my wolf better. It made things easier. Everyone said the better bond I had with my wolf, the easier the shifting would get and the less likely it was that he would just burst out when he or I got upset.

"Wolves are funny." Vash sat down between them. "Did I do the pancakes right? I burned the first two."

I stopped buttering my pancakes and looked at the bottom of them. They were golden brown, near perfection.

Harris laughed. "That might've been part of what threw your sense of smell off. There was a bit of smoke when I came in. Nothing we couldn't handle, right Vash?"

She shook her head and poured herself a bit of juice by levitating the bottle over to her cup. "Nope. Gavin helped me get everything just right. It's a big day, right?"

"Yeah." The first bite of pancakes nearly melted in my mouth. "First day of PTSD group, first full day of work, and if you and Vash are right, the first new client." They had both told me I'd get my first client on the same day we opened the office. Having people who could perceive things that were in the future was yet another thing I was getting accustomed to.

"Good. So Vash and I will meet you at the office after group, right?" Harris ran a hand down the most subdued tie-dyed T-shirt he owned. It was grays and blues as opposed to his normal bright yellows and reds.

I nodded, wishing I had time to eat a couple of stacks of the delicious pancakes. By far, it was Vash's best cooking effort yet. "That was the plan with Garnet. But if you're too busy, we can meet up somewhere else."

Harris pursed his lips as he chewed some bacon. "Nope, I'll make sure to point us that direction at about that time. We might be a few minutes late, but it shouldn't be a big problem."

Vash finished her sip of her juice and set her cup down. "I'll keep him on time. I've always been good with time."

"Thank you, Vash." Harris smiled and patted her hand. "Sometimes it's hard to remember that you're over two thousand years old, and not the eight that you look like."

The alarm I'd set on my phone went off. I grabbed the phone out of my jeans to turn it off. "Okay, I need to get." My pancakes were only half gone, but I couldn't help that.

I started out of the kitchen, then turned and went back to kiss the top of Vash's head. A wash of happy pinkish sparks danced down her ruddy locks. "Be good for Harris, okay?"

Vash nodded. "I will. See you later, Lucas."

"Thanks for filling in, Harris." I hurried down the hall, making sure to grab Stormbringer and the sword, that I hadn't named yet. The long sword still wasn't a weapon I was totally comfortable with, but Garnet, Harris, and Kilkari were all working with me and getting me a little better with it. Digger Urson, the alpha bear shifter in Denver who had made both weapons, said a name for the sword would come. The sword was specifically made to deal with Djinn. I didn't like leaving it around Vash, but since we'd had to deal with some Dark Djinn, Effrits, strategically, I liked having it nearby.

The hybrid Subaru hadn't been my first choice for a car, but of the SUVs and trucks we'd looked at, it had the least metal in its body. Vash was uncomfortable in vehicles with too much metal. That didn't make a lot of sense to anyone in our circle of friends, but we'd adjusted and I had a Subaru.

As I sped down the dirt road, I couldn't help but glance back over my shoulder toward the house. I knew Vash would be fine with Harris, but I kept flashing back to when the Effrits had stolen her while Garnet had been watching her. There was always the possibility that something would happen to the little Djinn girl who was meaning more and more to me every day.

2

Even though the VA center in Colorado Springs was a brand-new building, with all the shiny parts still glistening, I rapidly grew tired of going in. The place was almost too clean and smelled like it. Everyone kept telling me that as my wolf and I got to understand each other more, we'd come to understandings and part of that would help with what was occasionally over-taxed senses. Humans really have no idea how much they miss with the limited senses they're born with. My wolf senses were so keen I was often overwhelmed by the things that hit me. Luckily a wolf's vision is fairly close to humans', but hearing and smell were so much keener.

As I hurried into the foyer of the center, a pair of women were arguing softly about how they should let the VA know they were married. One was against it for fear of reprisals. Don't ask, don't tell still weighed heavily even on the retired military. The other was wanting the benefits they could gain if their marriage was acknowledged. Maybe my solitary love life had its advantages in more than just not having to deal with another person's wants and desires. I'd never had to try to explain things to the government.

A man brushed by me, reeking of pot smoke. The scent was enough to make me gag as I turned to try to locate the meeting room where my group was supposed to be starting. Even humans could pick up on pot smoke, and if people claimed otherwise, they were totally nose blind.

After a month of one-on-one meetings with a PTSD counselor, he'd decided I was safe to introduce to the one group that was run by an ex-Army man, Sergeant Santiago. I knew enough to understand that PTSD varied and was different for each person suffering from it. The things that triggered me off wouldn't be the same things that set other people off, but then how many people had to deal with their unit being torn apart by werewolves attacking during a sandstorm? Probably not many.

The elevator took me up to the second floor. A musky scent of dog filled the small metal box. I flashed to being in the Hummer after the werewolf had torn into my leg. The space was small. With deep breaths, I told myself I was going to be okay. I'd been in the elevator on previous trips to the center. I'd been fine. But there hadn't been the odor of dog. It was different from wolves but close, too close.

From inside me, my wolf growled.

The door opened and I rushed over to the railing that looked down into the foyer. For several seconds, I couldn't stop my hands from shaking as I gripped the railing.

Slow, deep breaths.

I pushed back against the wolf wanting to get

out and defend me from the irrational fear that welled up in me. Sometimes it was like I had no control at all. I hated it.

The elevator dinged and the doors slid open again.

More deep breaths. My wolf slowly retreated and went back to sleep.

A hand touched my shoulder.

I spun and pulled my fist back. My wolf was instantly awake and baring our teeth.

The large man jumped back and raised his hand in a placating gesture. "Sorry, Dude. You looked like you could use someone to talk to." His dark skin was pale and his hands shook slightly.

With another breath, I opened my hand and forced the wolf back down. I closed my eyes and shook my head. "No. Sorry. I just reacted."

He smiled. "I get it. None of us came back the same way we left."

I nodded. "Yeah. The elevator got to me. It hasn't before."

With a thumbs-up, he returned my nod. "Been there. Took me over a year before I could ride even one floor. They still make me feel like I'm trapped in the hold of a ship while it's sinking and things are exploding around me. If it's more than five floors, I take the stairs."

"Stairs are healthier." It was getting easier to relax.

"Where you going?"

"PTSD group." It was also getting easier to tell strangers I had a problem. I hated showing weakness.

"Me too." He waved down the hall. "Come on, we're about to be late."

"Sure." I took another slow breath and we headed down the hall to a mostly empty room, no desks or walls, just a circle of chairs, only half of them occupied. Several of the men there had dogs at their sides or feet. That explained the scent of dog in the elevator. I started to wonder if the group session was going to be a good idea.

All four of the dogs stiffened and stared at me as I walked in. The concentrated attention made me more nervous than the attention of humans would've. I knew how to deal with humans, but I wasn't always sure how to deal with animals. The dogs knew I wasn't human, and I waited for them to react. They glanced at each other. They had a pecking order that had nothing to do with the humans at their sides. A couple of them looked up at their humans, but the men were already watching me and the other man walk in and none of them paid attention to their dogs' nervousness.

"Come in, come in," said the shorter man who stood near the window.

I took a few steps in then stopped, staring at the short man with shoulder-length black hair. "Santiago?"

He'd been turning around, then stopped and gave me more than a passing glance. "Corporal Lucas?"

"That's Sergeant Lucas, soldier." I laughed. I hadn't seen Theodore Santiago since basic training. We'd bunked next to each other for almost three months before getting deployed to different countries.

"What are you doing in Colorado Springs?" Santiago took several quick strides to me and held out his hand.

I grasped his offered hand. It felt good to see a familiar face. "Got dumped here and decided to stay. I'm not too far from family." It was a good cover story. A lot of soldiers just stayed where they got out, and it was easier than explaining that a werewolf in the FBI told me I was going to stay here for my own good and learn from the local pack. Not that the magical oath that protected the supernatural community would've let me explain that to a non-magical human.

"I heard the air was cleaner around here." Santiago let go of my hand and grinned. "They lied. But, I like it. How long have you been here?" At his side, a large German shepherd bristled but didn't bark or growl. It watched me as if daring me to do something to Santiago so it could try to tear my throat out.

As much as my wolf wanted to growl at the dog, warning him we weren't something he wanted to mess with, I pushed the urge down. Santiago was a friend, and that meant his support dog was too. I'd heard that some of the guys who had major issues with their PTSD had support animals, but hadn't encountered one until that point.

"I've been here nearly three months."

"Just getting settled."

"Yeah. Officially opening my security office today, so I guess that's settled."

Santiago waved over to the chairs. "You'll have

to tell me more later. We need to get started."

"Definitely." I deliberately picked a chair that was as far away from anyone with a dog as possible. I figured it was a good way to keep from causing disruptions. Sure, they all had the support dog vests on and should've been highly trained, but I didn't want to take any chances.

Standing in an opening in the chairs, Santiago whistled. "Okay, guys let's get started." Until that moment, I hadn't realized he was our group leader. He'd never struck me as the most understanding guy in the world. In basic, he'd been just slightly above average and missed getting into the Rangers by just a hair in his marksmanship tests.

"Since we've got a couple of new guys, let's take a minute and go around the room and introduce ourselves. If you're comfortable with it, tell us why you're here." Santiago settled into his chair, and his dog lay down at his side, but never took his attention off me. It's gaze was more intense than any dog I'd ever met.

"I'll start. I'm Lieutenant Theo Santiago. I have severe PTSD. Five years ago, my unit was in Iraq and we drove over some IEDs. We lost five good men. I got lucky and came out of it whole, after spending six weeks in the hospital to repair a punctured lung and seven broken ribs. As long as I keep my shirt on, nobody can see my scars, but I can still hear the men of my unit dying." He reached down and rubbed his dog's head.

I understood where he was coming from. The screams of my unit as the werewolves tore into them still woke me up at night in a cold sweat. There were times I wanted the dreams to end, and other times I hoped they never would. I didn't want to forget they'd died and I'd made it out alive…changed but alive.

"Oh," Santiago continued as he kept on petting his dog's head. "This is Worf, he's my guardian warrior. He keeps me centered and chases the evil away."

A couple of the people in the room chuckled. One woman with her own service dog, a dog that looked like it was a cross between a golden retriever and a cattle dog, nodded and clapped.

Then we moved on to the guy on Santiago's left. It took several minutes before it was my turn. Everyone had tales of either battle scars or abuse in various arms of the military.

The man I'd met outside the elevator was Admiral Steve Perkins, former Navy, who'd been on a ship that had been sunk in the Arabian Sea. He'd suffered badly but didn't have a service animal due to allergies. With a laugh, he said his wife was his service animal.

Several of the men laughed, but the two women in the circle glared at him. I knew there was a lot of misogyny in the military and did my best to ignore it when I could. It didn't help things get better, but I always had other things to worry about while I'd been in the system, and being out, I had to worry about Vash and the world we lived in. Maybe, once things settled down, it would be something to start working against. Women were people too, and all lives mattered.

Then it was my turn. "Hi, I'm Sergeant David

Lucas. A few months back, my unit of Army Rangers ran over a series of IEDs during a series of sandstorms in Afghanistan. Before we could make it back to base, we got hit by insurgents. I was the only one to make it out." I shuddered. The story wasn't totally accurate, but it was the closest I could get. Humans couldn't know about the supernatural world. It wasn't allowed and there were spells in place to prevent it from happening. But the story was the *official* version of what happened. As the people around me had poured out their pain, I had to toe the official line and it sucked. "I can't handle tight spaces, howling, or crowds. I keep dreaming of what happened."

Santiago looked at me and cocked his head. "Howling? That's a new one. Any idea why howling?"

I shrugged. "While I was trying to find my way back to base, there were wolves or something that seemed to be following me. I never saw them, but could hear them at night."

"Must have been jackals," one of the women we hadn't gotten to yet offered up. "I don't think there's wolves in Afghanistan, but jackals are a lot like coyotes. Howling and yipping."

"Maybe." I leaned forward and put my elbows on my knees. "I haven't done any research on it."

She smiled my direction. "Tell you what, I'll look into it and let you know next week."

"Thanks." I nodded but didn't smile back. Although I'd probably make friends in the group, most people did in similar situations, I didn't need the complications of having too many humans around. If Agent Briar hadn't been so insistent about me going to PTSD counseling, I wouldn't have been sitting there. He'd been pretty adamant about dealing with the human side of things as well as the wolf side. He kept threatening to put me out of my misery if I didn't get things under control. If he had to do that, Vash would be locked away in her bell and stored somewhere she couldn't be turned into a powerful weapon. There was no way I was going to allow that to happen, so I was sitting there in counseling.

After everyone went through their introductions, we spent the remainder of the hour-long session discussing things the group members had encountered since the last meeting and what they'd done to deal with them, or how they'd felt about not dealing with them. Some of them were support buddies and called each other when things got out of control. Overall, it was an interesting hour, but even though I could sympathize with them, my situation was so different, I wasn't sure I'd get much out of the meetings. I couldn't get a support animal and wasn't sure about having a support buddy. I had Kilkari, Summers, the badger up the mountain, and Harris to call when things got rough on the werewolf side of things, and that was really harder to deal with than the regular human emotions.

As the group broke up, Santiago walked over. Worf came slowly at his side, keeping his eyes down but observant, waiting for me to make a dangerous move. Santiago held out a card. "Here's my info. Call or email me and we can go get coffee or dinner sometime. It would be good to catch up."

I nodded and pulled out my wallet, taking out the new cards I'd just received for my security firm. "Sure." I took his card and handed him one of mine. "That would be great."

He looked at my card and chuckled. "Watching Wolf Security in Black Forest. I like it. Are you going for the big bad wolf motif?"

"Sure." I shrugged. Vash, Harris, and I had debated the name for a while, and Kilkari had said he liked it. Animal themed businesses were hot in Colorado, he'd said. I stuck Santiago's card in my wallet without really looking at it.

"Cool. Well, Worf and I have an appointment to get his nails done, so we've got to get rolling. Like I said if you need anything call." Santiago held out his hand again.

I shook it.

Worf looked up at me from a bowed head and pulled his lips away from his fangs looking like he was about to pounce.

My wolf wanted to return the look, and I forced him back. "You guys have fun. I'm heading to the office."

On my way out of the building, I took the stairs next to the elevator, as it was better than being in the enclosed space full of dog scent. I still had a long way to go. With luck, the rest of the day was going to be without unexpected things like support dogs and facing other people's battle-related fears.

3

A surreal feeling washed over me as I unlocked the simple glass door to Watching Wolf Security. It was my business. I had never expected to open a business, let alone a security firm. When I sat down and was honest with myself and others, I hadn't really planned much beyond surviving my time as a Ranger. Yeah, I'd put most of the money back, but hadn't had a defined trail when I stopped and thought about things. I never claimed to be the sharpest tack in the box. So there I stood, and opened the door to the first business I had, and like being a father to Vash, or being a werewolf, I had little idea of what I was really doing.

The scent of smoke hit me seconds before Vash called my name. "Lucas!" She dashed down the sidewalk toward me. Her body was a little more indistinct than it should've been, but when she got excited, she sometimes still had trouble staying solid.

Warm fuzzy happy feelings hit me as she wrapped her arms around my stomach and hugged me. She was holding back on her sparks, which was good.

I bent slightly and hugged her back. "Hey,

Vash."

"We brought donuts." Harris held up a flat pink box and grinned. "Thought it would be a good opening day treat."

I grinned as I straightened. Vash kept her arms around me. "Thanks, Harris. I'm new at this business thing. Had no clue."

He shrugged as I pushed the door open so we could go in. "Every business is different. Can't say as I know anyone in the security business, so I just guessed."

"There were lots of choices." Vash took the box and carried it over the counter where the coffee pot sat waiting to be turned on. "I've never heard of a lot of them. Gavin let me pick out some that sounded good." She opened the box and pulled out one that had a swirl of pink and blue frosting and a bit of sugary floss around the top. "What is cotton candy?"

Although her question made sense, I had to laugh. I never knew when Vash was going to come off sounding very adult, and when she was going to act like a child a little younger than the eight she appeared. "Try it. I used to eat a ton of it, particularly when we went to the fair."

"State fair, or Renaissance Faire?" Harris cocked his head.

"I've never been to a Renaissance Fair," I replied. I watched Vash as she opened her mouth and took a bite out of the donut.

"We'll fix that next summer." Harris sat in one of the high-backed leather chairs I'd bought for clients. There were two set in front of my large dark wooden desk. The whole place looked a bit fancier than I was used to.

"It's very sweet." Vash wiped a bit of cotton candy off her chin. "I think I like it."

"Good." Harris looked like he was going to say something else, but a distant look crossed his face. Then he stood up. "I hate to rush off, but there's something odd."

"Need help?" I often offered to lend Harris a hand at various things, but he was good at deflecting the offers.

He raised a hand and shook his head. "Nah, it's just something magical. Odds are it's nothing. I'll check back in with you later."

It wouldn't do me any good to argue. Odds were Vash and I would just spend the day sitting waiting for either the phone to ring or an email to show up. "Okay. Thanks for covering for me while I was in group." It didn't bother me to say I was in therapy, at least with Harris. I was screwed up and had the supernatural world to thank for that. Between PTSD and being a turned werewolf, I had a lot of adjusting to do, and just asking people for help was a big thing for me. I hated it, but it was my life.

"No worries." Harris ruffled Vash's hair as he headed for the door. "Vash and I get along great, don't we, Vash?"

Vash finished off her donut and grinned up at him. "Sure do." She gave him a quick hug. "We'll see you later."

"Hadn't planned on it, but maybe." Harris returned her hug, then hurried out, frowning slightly as he opened the door and headed for his car.

I looked at Vash. "Do you think we'll see Harris

again today?" Sometimes she seemed to know things she shouldn't. If I was honest with people, Vash had found my office space. We'd been driving past the strip center on the way home from Colorado Springs and she'd wanted to stop. It wasn't a large space but was perfect for what I needed.

She glanced out into the parking lot where Harris' car was heading toward the street. "Maybe. Hard to really say. Time moves of its own accord." And there was the older child who was really over two thousand years old even if she'd only spent about eight years outside the bell to which she was bound.

"Then we'll just have to wait and see." I stepped behind my desk and turned on the computer as I settled in the seat. The plush leather chair squeaked slightly as my weight settled into it. It felt more like something I should be getting comfortable in to watch TV, rather than a desk chair, but when Garnet and Cin Kilkari had helped me buy office furniture, they'd both assured me it would make a good impression on clients. The fresh leather smell engulfed me. It made me relax just a bit.

"You look important back there." Vash hopped up into the chair Harris had used. "People will be impressed with you."

"You've been listening to Cin and Garnet again, haven't you?" The computer's splash-screen came on, then seconds later, my business logo, a classic howling wolf with a full-moon behind it, appeared on the monitor.

"They are both full of useful information that is helping me adapt to the new time I live in." Vash gestured toward the donut box and a pastry floated up.

"Vash," I kept the growl in my voice low. "No magic in the office. We've got huge windows."

Frowning, she turned and looked out the windows as the donut returned to its box. "They are large and someone with sharp eyes might see from the parking lot. I'm sorry, Lucas."

"It's okay." I got up and retrieved the donut she'd been floating, grabbed one for myself, and took hers over. "We've both got a lot of learning to do."

My computer beeped with an incoming email.

Vash's frown vanished as I handed her the pastry. "Thank you, Lucas. I could've gotten up. The guardian isn't supposed to serve the Djinn."

Biting into my donut, I waved the comment away. "It's no problem, Vash. And we've talked about the serving thing." Djinn apparently were historically nearly slaves to the person who held onto the item they were bound to. Their items, the bell in Vash's case, were also their prisons. Since I'd freed Vash, I'd never forced her back to her bell, although she'd retreated there from time to time when she had overdone her magic.

"This world is confusing at times." She took a bite out of the marshmallow-covered sweet.

Returning to my seat, I expected to find a well-wishing message from one of our new friends, but I didn't recognize the name on the email. I clicked on it.

The email was short and simple.

Hello, I would like to know when you can

**come to my home and give me a security review.
Please call to set up a time.**

I stared at the screen. It wasn't how I envisioned my first client coming to me, but the modern world was a change for me like it was for Vash. There had been changes during the time I'd been enlisted. Trying to get used to them, I pulled out my cellphone and made the call. I didn't want to make someone willing to pay for my expertise wait. Might as well get the new life off and running.

4

"This voice who guides us is incredible." Vash picked up my phone and looked at it as we turned off the highway and angled toward Manitou Springs. "I know you and Garnet keep telling me that there's no Djinn bound to the cell phones, and I don't feel magic coming from them, but they are just odd."

I laughed. Vash's naiveté was refreshing when I compared her to other people I knew who had grown up with technology and just accepted it as part of our lives. "To many people, particularly older folks, or poorer people, the AI tech can seem very magical."

Vash shook her head as the techno voice advised another turn that took us back under the highway and toward Garden of the Gods. "If there is magic in this, it is something totally tied to humans."

We took a left at a Y in the road and seconds later came to a massive, beautifully-crafted steel gate, with worked ivy and roses that glistened in the sunlight, and looked like it could keep a rampaging rhino out. The wall on either side of the gate was at least eight feet tall and two feet thick. The entrance was designed to keep people out. I rolled down the Outback's window and leaned out to enter the code the client had given me when I had called and set up the appointment. After a moment, the gate swung open and the AI advised us that we were entering a private community. I didn't really need her input to know that.

Along our path were more gates and walls, though none as impressive as the main gate. Most of them appeared to be more decorative than anything. Here and there, as the road twisted, the burn scar where we'd last fought the Effrit, who'd stolen Vash a few months back, came into view. The last time I had been in the area, we'd been on a road that ran along the top of the canyon the subdivision was in. I wondered if it was a sign, a warning. Hopefully not. Vash and I didn't need trouble. I needed the job.

Two more turns and a short straightaway, and we arrived at the address. Another wall, a little more formidable than the others we'd passed since coming into the development rose up. It was painted a reddish-brown to match the monolith stones of Garden of the Gods.

The gate swung open as we approached. It just took a glance for me to see the camera halfway up the wall between the gate and the top of the wall. I pulled through the opening slowly and caught the glint of light indicating a smaller camera that was little more than a bump on the top of the wall.

Vash glanced around. "Lucas, there is magic here."

"What kind?" I didn't react, in case more cameras were watching us. A good soldier never gave away something simple and telling that might warn a potential enemy they knew of their presence.

"Nothing major." Vash frowned. "I think

someone put a ward on the gate. I don't recognize the kind of magic. It's not Djinn, or human, like Gavin and Garnet practice."

I'd planned on leaving her in the car while I went in, but I wasn't so sure. As I pulled up the winding drive, the house appeared to come out of the hill. From above, it might even blend into the stones, dirt, and natural scrub of the hillside. There were a couple of cars, all small sports cars and electric vehicles, no trucks or SUVs, which struck me as odd in Colorado. People in the Springs loved their trucks and SUVs.

"Will you be okay out here?" I turned off the car and looked over at Vash.

She nodded. "I believe so. If not, I will retreat to my bell. You have it on you."

It wasn't a question. I hadn't failed to put the bell in my pocket every day since she'd first come out of it. In some ways, it was my most precious possession. If I died and the bell fell into the wrong hands, Vash's life would be hell, and I wasn't about to let that happen.

"Okay." I pulled out the keys after rolling the windows down. "If you spot anything odd, let me know when I get back."

"Of course." She nodded, then pulled out the tablet I'd gotten her.

As I got out of the car, I hoped she wasn't going to be doing any online shopping. Garnet and Cin had introduced her to it, and every so often she still did a little without telling me first. I'd put dollar limits on my Amazon account and that helped.

Before I could worry too much, the front door

opened and a tall, well groomed, well-dressed man looked out at me. "Mr. Lucas, thank you for coming." The sunlight seemed to play along his long platinum hair and pale blue eyes. He had the smoothest, and most unblemished skin I'd ever seen. A few months earlier and I'd have said it was uncanny, but it took more than perfect skin to hit me as odd.

"Mr. Alford." I made it up the concrete steps and across the sweeping porch before offering the man my hand.

Alford's handshake was a little weaker than I was used to, and he nodded. "Your hand shows you're used to hard work. That's nice to know." He looked me over. "Yes, I believe your profile on your business site was correct. That's refreshing. So many people aren't opposed to embellishing their background when they think it will benefit them." Then his gaze traveled to the Subaru parked next to the Tesla convertible. There was the barest hint of interest, then he looked back at me. "Please come in, we can get started."

"Thanks, but I already started. I noticed two cameras at the front gate. The small one is a nice touch." I pointed back down the drive.

"Yes." Alford smiled. It was an easy look on him, and from the lines that appeared around his eyes, one he used often. "But there were a couple of others as well. We can walk out there and let you see what you think unless you'd rather look around the house first."

I stopped the frown that tried to form before it could show. More cameras? They must be well hidden. That would be good for defense. "That's up to you. We can start wherever you like."

A thoughtful look crossed Alford's face, then he nodded. "Yes, let's go out and check the gate first. Beyond the community gate, it is my personal first line of defense. I must confess, recently some less than desirable people have moved into the neighborhood, and the main gate won't keep *them* from me."

After having driven through the neighborhood, I wasn't sure I wanted to know what he considered 'less than desirable'. Maybe someone who won their fortune through the lotto wasn't as desirable as someone who inherited theirs or made it through one of the many tech startups.

We started down the steps, and taking a bit slower, I felt a tingle along my leg as I broke a laser beam that wasn't visible in the sunlight. Depending on how it was set up, it probably wouldn't be obvious at night either. I paused and glanced across the steps. The barest indention in the concrete revealed where the laser came from.

I walked over and knelt. "Laser beam here. That's a good warning heading in."

"Right." Alford smiled again and nodded. "You *are* good. Most people wouldn't spot that during the day."

"I didn't survive several tours in the Middle East by missing things like that." It would've been a complete newbie mistake, but more than a few units had lost good men to such things over the years.

"Of course."

When I straightened, another indentation, this

time in a concrete flower urn, drew my eye. I strode over and passed my hand over the spot a couple of times to make sure it wasn't another laser, then looked at the camera lens just under the concrete edge. I'd heard that cameras were getting smaller and smaller, but was amazed how something little bigger than a pen cap could have enough space to hold everything a camera needed to operate. "Another camera."

"Very good. I do have nearly every inch of my property covered by surveillance. We'll go to the control room after we get finished with your inspection of the yard." Alford waved us down the driveway.

For the next half-hour, we walked around the outside of his house. He had cameras of various sizes, shapes, and concealments every few feet. Along the driveway, they were in urns, statues, and rocks. They were built into the perimeter wall, some had little access ports, and others didn't. There were more lasers too. A couple of the larger cameras on the gate wall also held lasers, and from what I could tell, those were more than just warning bells but defensive. A couple of the statues along the drive, huge concrete archers, also had defensive lasers.

"I have to say, I wouldn't want to try to storm your home, Mr. Alford." I cast one last look over the yard as we headed into the house.

"I'm glad to hear that." Alford shook his head, his long hair whipped around him. "Hopefully the new neighbors will think twice about it too. Now…"

"Now you're going to let the poor man rest." A woman stood in the foyer. Like Alford, she was tall and elegant. Where some of his edges were sharp, hers were softer. Her hair was a coppery match to his platinum. Her eyes green to his icy blue. They felt like different seasons housed in the same home.

"Mr. Lucas is here for business, my dear." Mr. Alford paused. "Mr. Lucas, forgive my wife, she's always ready to make sure our hearth is open to all who stop by."

"And business associates should be welcomed hospitably, my husband." Mrs. Alford's smile reminded me of sunlight on autumn leaves. "Please, Mr. Lucas, go get your daughter and join us for a bit of lemonade. I just bought the lemons this morning at the farmer's market."

I hadn't intended to involve Vash in the job, but Mrs. Alford had either been watching out the window or on the many cameras. When I glanced at Mr. Alford, he had a resigned, and slightly hen-pecked look as he spread his hands in resignation. "All right. Give me a moment and I'll go get Vash." There was something about her words that caught me as odd, but I couldn't put my finger on it. They were more than they seemed, but I couldn't be sure what.

Mrs. Alford arched a rusty eyebrow. "Vash, very pretty and unusual name."

Without responding, I went out to the car. "Vash, you've been invited in for some lemonade."

She looked up from her tablet. "Is it okay?"

Without turning to look at the house, I nodded. "I think so. Have you felt any more magic?"

"A little." She put her tablet on the console between the seats. "But nothing horrible. I think they're using the roses to keep something out, but the only things roses really keep out are vampires. Do we have vampires around?"

"Yes." Although we hadn't met any, Harris and Kilkari both said there were some in Denver.

"Okay." Vash undid her seat belt, then got out and rushed around to me. There weren't any sparks trailing after her, a sign she was working on keeping her glamor going. "Maybe they're afraid of vampires."

After Alford's comments about less than desirables, I figured that would fit the bill. I'd check my sources and see if anyone knew of vampires living in the subdivision, although I wasn't sure if cameras, lasers, and roses would be enough to keep vampires out. It might be a good idea for me to do a bit of research on them and find out.

Vash took my hand, then paused as we started up the steps. "Do I look nice enough to meet your clients?"

I chuckled. Garnet and Cin were rubbing off on her. "Yes, Vash, you're very pretty."

She beamed. "Thanks, Lucas."

Although I still wasn't sure about taking her in with me, it was a job. After all, I was suddenly a little more on watch as we walked across the porch. I was almost positive I'd found every laser and camera on the place. We were safe. I'd been asked out to make sure the property was secure. To that point, I hadn't found anything that said otherwise.

I paused at the door, glancing around to make sure there wasn't something I'd missed, something that might be a danger to Vash.

"It's okay." Vash took my hand before opening the door. "We're fine here."

It was hard to knock the feeling back that there was something that I'd missed. Something important.

5

"I'm not used to missing important things." Harris stomped into our living room and whirled around.

Before I could get the door closed, Garnet came in after him. "Lucas, see if you can get him to calm down. I've been with him since school let out, and I can't."

I glanced out the door to make sure there wasn't anyone else on my porch waiting to come in. It looked like it was clear. Once the door was closed, I turned to look at Harris who was pacing the living room. I was tempted to tell him he was the human and I was the werewolf, wolves pace, humans should be able to resist the urge, but his face had a hard set to it that didn't look like he was ready for a bit of levity.

Before I could say anything, Vash came in from the hall. "Gavin. Garnet. I thought I felt you both come in." She rushed over and hugged Garnet.

"Hey, Sweety." Garnet hugged her, then kissed her head.

A shower of bright happy golden sparks floated from Vash's hair and swirled around both of them before disappearing inches from the hardwood floor.

Vash turned and looked at Harris. "What's wrong, Gavin, you're agitated."

Harris shook his head. "I can't find the strange magic I felt earlier. It's like it was there and then vanished."

I strode over and leaned against the doorframe heading into the kitchen. "And this is unusual? Wouldn't you have the sensation if it was a teleporter? You know, like Vash can do."

"Or someone using a portal," Garnet suggested. "I've asked the same thing."

"But it didn't feel like that." Harris ran his fingers through his shoulder-length pale blond hair. "I know what teleporters feel like. They just pop in and out, leaving only a hint of a sensation in their wake."

"Like the bit of sulfur in the air after a bullet's fired?" I offered, trying to make sense of something I wasn't sure I understood.

Pausing, Harris got thoughtful for a moment, then he smiled. "Yeah, good analogy. But what I felt wasn't like that. It was there, strong as could be, and then it was just gone. I've been driving around for hours and just can't pick up on anything like it. Although I did find out that the family of Trolls has moved back into that little space under the highway near America the Beautiful park."

"Trolls?" I stared at Harris. "Trolls are real?" I really hated not having all the intel on the supernatural world. If I wasn't spending so much time trying to sort myself out, maybe I'd have the spare bandwidth to learn more before things came hurtling out of the darkness and smacked me in the side of the head.

"Yeah, most of the fairy tales are, to one extent or another." Garnet had settled on the couch with Vash sitting tight against her.

Vash nodded. "Trolls can be rather nasty, but then they aren't as complicated as humans are."

Harris laughed. "Complicated. Are all Djinn as diplomatic as you are, Vash? Most people would just call Trolls stupid and be done with it."

"No, but Cin said it isn't polite to call people stupid in this time." Vash smiled. "I am trying to fit in."

"And you're doing a great job, Sweety." Garnet gave her another hug.

"You're fitting in better than a lot of people who were born here." Harris turned toward me. "So, Lucas, what are you and Vash doing tomorrow?"

I shrugged. "Hanging out in the office and waiting for someone to stop by or call." I figured when I didn't have a client that was what we were going to be doing most days.

"Can you and Vash, or just Vash come and help me search? Vash's magical senses are a lot more sensitive than mine. She might pick up on something that Garnet or I might miss."

Tracking down magic wasn't something I was used to doing. I glanced at Vash. "What do you think, Vash? Can you track something Harris can't?"

A thoughtful line crossed Vash's forehead, then she nodded. "Yes, my senses are stronger than most humans. I should be able to spot things he missed."

My phone beeped with an incoming email. Figuring the only thing we had left to sort out was timing. I raised a finger. "Let me check this, make sure it's not another client."

Harris nodded. "Sure."

I pulled up the message. It was from Sergeant Santiago.

Lucas, After suggesting we get coffee or something, I'm being called out of town. I'll let you know when I get back. I might miss our next group meeting but have arranged for a stand-in if that happens.

Closing the message and turning off the screen, I slipped the phone back into my pocket. "Nothing major. So when are we leaving in the morning?"

Harris shot Garnet a glance.

She shook her head. "Don't look at me. I've got another round of subbing tomorrow. I'll be teaching art classes all week."

"Okay. I forgot." Harris turned to me. "So that's up to you. Still getting out of bed with the chickens?"

Years of being up at the crack of dawn, or before, and often having days stretch past midnight had warped my sleep patterns to the point that they were often very chaotic. "Tell me when and we'll be up."

"Werewolves and Djinn don't need as much sleep as humans." Vash sounded much like an encyclopedia, or wiki listing.

"Then let's say about six. I did manage to narrow things down to a couple of spots. We can start there. One of them is up near where we fought the Effrits out Rampart Range Road, but it didn't feel like it was right there."

I looked at Vash. "Is there any chance the bit of magic you felt at the Alford house could've been a portal or teleportation?"

She looked thoughtful, then frowned slightly. "No. That magic was designed to keep things out. Wards only, a portal would be much stronger."

"Okay, I'm still getting the hang of all this magic stuff." But remembering the Alfords reminded me of what I wanted to ask Harris about. "Harris, are there vampires in the area?"

"Denver," he blurted out almost instantly. "Like the werewolves, the vampires have the state seat in Denver. Actually, I think Lord Morningstar oversees this part of the western U.S. The coven there was a bit larger before they had some infighting a year or so back. That left a good number of them dead. Luckily it didn't last too long, or the rest of the supernatural community would've gotten involved to keep them from drawing unwanted attention. The Oath only works to a certain point, and if we start having a war in the streets, humans are going to figure out what's going on. Do you think your new clients were vampires?"

I shook my head. "Not so much. They'd mentioned something about undesirables moving into their subdivision and wanting to make sure their defenses were good. Vash said some of the rose bushes might be filling gaps to keep vampires out."

"Roses are good for that, yes." Harris sighed. "I can make some calls and find out if Morningstar has let part of his court expand this direction. If they have, it would've been polite for him to warn me about their arrival."

Although I could see where it was a good idea for different supernaturals to warn the locals about expansion plans and such, there was always the possibility there was more to sending in a small group to feel out the area. I'd seen it with insurgents, send in a couple of people disguised as refugees into an unsuspecting community, and then pretty soon 'family' starts coming in and before anyone realizes the village has been taken over. With my retirement from the Army, I thought I was done with such things, but it looked like I'd just traded one form of drama for another.

"Thanks." I grinned. "Hey, Vash and I were about to throw some steaks on the grill, would you two like some? I got them from the butcher in Monument. Great place."

Harris glanced at his high priestess.

Garnet laughed. "Sure. We didn't bring anything to contribute, but I can help with some of the prep."

"Or you can come sit in the kitchen and entertain us while we fix dinner." I straightened from the doorframe. "You fixed us plenty of dinners while we were getting settled."

"I shouldn't stay out too late." Garnet grinned as she and Vash got off the couch. "Gotta make sure the kids get their art sub tomorrow."

Vash paused and seemed to study Garnet. "Maybe you can teach me art, so I can do it myself and it lasts longer than a day."

"That would be fun." Garnet laughed.

"It would be." Vash joined her laughter.

Although Vash never seemed to look at it as a

drawback, her Djinn magic only lasted a day, if that. Anything she created with her magic vanished with the sunrise the next day. From what Harris said, it was a way to limit the power the Djinns had, but I wondered if it was something more. There were still a lot of things I didn't know about magic and the creatures who used it,

"For now, let's make a salad while Lucas and Gavin get the steaks going." Garnet stopped a couple of feet from me and shooed me toward the kitchen.

Strong, dominant people, even the supernatural had a pecking order, and I'd found myself sitting in the middle of a bunch of the people who were at the top of it. In a lot of ways, it was like sitting in a room full of generals, but luckily, these normally got along and weren't opposed to getting their hands dirty.

I gave Garnet a slight bow, then went through the kitchen and out the back door to the porch where the coals were just getting to the point they'd get steaks good and done. Accepting the idea that there were vampires in the area, I thought back to the Alfords. Could they have been something other than human and I just missed it? Sure, as a werewolf I had a sharp nose, but if I didn't know what I was smelling, would I have known it was dangerous? I needed to learn more, experience more if I was going to keep Vash safe from the supernaturals we shared the world with.

6

I turned the Outback in the direction Harris wanted me to go, deeper into the foothills west of Castle Rock. The gently rolling landscape kept promising to get into something steeper, but the roads he directed me down turned away from getting into the mountains just minutes to the west. When we'd been house hunting, there had been a couple of trips into the area, but after enduring childhood winters in Montana, I wasn't sure about wintering in higher, steeper lands, at least not until I saw things were going to pan out.

"Up that way." Harris pointed down a dirt road I was nearly past.

Jamming on the breaks, I was thankful that, for the first time in about half an hour, there wasn't anyone on my tail. That was another thing I didn't really like in the area, too many cars, and people.

Vash braced herself against the back of my seat, not that an accident could hurt her much, she'd probably go all smoky and get out of any wreck we had.

Spinning the wheel, I headed the direction Harris wanted to go. "Finally heading into the mountains?"

Harris shrugged. "Hard to tell. I tend to avoid this area. Not really sure why. It's like something, maybe the land itself, doesn't appreciate magic users around here."

"Okay, this is more of my magical learning curve." I kept my speed a little lower than the posted limit as the ruts in the road were a bit more extreme than I liked. "But what does that even mean?"

"It's odd, actually. Some areas have things like ley lines, and other natural magical phenomena that are welcoming to magic users, or magic users of certain kinds, like druids and such," Harris immediately dropped into lecture mode.

I held up a hand. "And see, the different kinds of magic users haven't been explained to me either, and honestly, I don't really care. Vash is a Djinn, her magic is all I need to understand at this point."

"And her magic is a bit more advanced than most of the human magic you're going to find." Harris sighed. "But you're right, you don't need to know all about different kinds of magic. When I said this area seems to dislike magic or dissuade us, it's like there is a bit of a vacuum here. I can't totally explain it. Think of a black hole in the night sky. There should be magic, lots of it in the area, but there's nothing."

A bit of movement in the backseat drew my attention to the rearview mirror.

Vash was nodding. "He's right. There's an absence here. Mountains and such are normally full of magic."

"So that in itself is a potential problem." And that was something I understood. It was like going through a village where potential terrorists might be hiding and realizing that the only people on the street were Americans. It was a sure sign something was up, normally something dangerous.

"Exactly." Harris pointed toward a hill about a mile away. "It seems to be worse over there."

"I agree." Vash patted his shoulder.

"Then let's head that way." I turned left at the next road. Although I wasn't thrilled about the idea of taking Vash with us while looking for potential trouble, Harris had been right, her magical senses were stronger than his.

Vash started tapping my shoulder. "Lucas, stop!"

Again, I jammed on the breaks, sliding a bit more on the dirt than I had on the pavement of the highway we'd been on when Harris had me turn. "What's up?" Once we were stopped, I looked over my shoulder and she wasn't in the backseat any more.

My pulse raced as I stared at Harris. "What just happened? Where is she?"

Harris was glancing about frantically. "She teleported out of the car."

With a growl, I slammed the Subaru into park and threw my door opened. "Vash!" My wolf surged forward; he was as protective as her as I was, and his senses were stronger.

"Over here." Her voice was only slightly raised.

As the whiff of fragrant smoke and ash hit me, I spotted her leaning across a fence reaching for a camel on the other side. Her lower half was nearly transparent like she was having trouble holding herself together. Excited bright yellow sparks cascaded around her.

I dashed across the short distance to her. "Vash, solid." I hadn't had to remind her to not be smoke in a couple of weeks.

Although she didn't say anything about it, her legs solidified and the glamour that hid her sparks shrouded her head. "Lucas, look, it's an ustra. You didn't tell me there were ustra here."

"Ustra?" I stared at the camel. "You mean the camel?"

She turned and looked at me and the beast came toward us. A thoughtful line crossed her forehead, then she nodded. "Yes, that is your word. Camel. Isn't she magnificent? One of the bearers of my bell back in time traded me to a merchant for three camels. He needed transportation more than the communication with his family that I could provide. They are so important. I was worried I'd never see one again. So much has changed in the world."

Harris laughed as he caught up with us. He held out the car keys. "Vash, we're going to have to take you to the zoo."

The camel got close enough for Vash to touch it. "The zoo?" She held out her hand so the camel could sniff her. "What is a zoo?"

I took the keys and jammed them into my pocket, relaxing a little as Vash stroked the camel's muzzle. "It's a park where lots of animals are kept. Things people don't often see in our modern world. You'd enjoy it." I wasn't exactly sure how the animals in the zoo would react to a werewolf wandering the sidewalks there. It might draw a bit more attention to my differences than I wanted. Although I'd love watching Vash in the strange environment, being a little girl, it might be safer if someone else took her. I'd check with Chad to see if either he or any of the other shifters he knew had tried going to a zoo, and if it would be safe.

As if reading my mind, Harris nodded and leaned against the wooden fence. "Let me talk to Garnet and we'll see about taking you sometime soon. You'll enjoy it."

With a huff, the camel shot me a hard look.

"I like animals, but I bet they don't like you, Lucas." Vash bent over and tore a clump of grass out and held it up for the camel.

"Which I bet was why Harris suggested that he and Garnet take you to the zoo." I took a few steps back to give the camel some space, but continued to keep an eye on Vash. Luckily, we were on a back road that didn't appear to have much traffic, and I didn't need to worry about stopping in the middle of the road.

"Oh, yes, that would be an alternative." Vash patted the camel as she finished off the grass. "Then I guess I need to find this strange energy in exchange for that."

Sometimes the way she put things together was amazing. Somehow the way she'd so calmly talked about being traded for a camel, and then popping off with the idea of working in exchange for something like a trip to the zoo reminded me both of the culture she'd…grown up in wasn't exactly the right word, but it was the closest I could come up with.

As we turned and headed toward the car, a big

red truck with jacked up suspension roared past. The driver rolled down the window and flipped us off.

Harris chuckled. "Guess he didn't like us just leaving the car sitting in the middle of the road. Just because it's a dirt road doesn't mean there isn't any traffic on it."

"I guess you're right." I wasn't about to admit that I often got pissed at drivers who did the same thing, and I defaulted to the thought process of lack of traffic meant I could do anything I wanted. My own brother would've probably given me what for.

When we got going again, Vash turned in her seat and watched as the camel disappeared over the hill. I'd never seen her react like that to something before, but then, other than the Effrits who'd wanted to kill her, we hadn't encountered anything from her past life.

The road climbed out of the valley and we leveled out for a short distance before the road climbed again.

"Over there," Harris and Vash said in unison as Harris pointed toward a hillside that looked a little more gray than green. A short road led the way over there and ended in a trash-filled pull out that looked like it might've been a trailhead at one point, but had seen better days. Even the trees were warped and twisted. I half-expected to have magical insurgents step out from behind the trees and attack us. The wolf inside me felt like it turned around and sat, waiting for the unexpected to rush toward us.

"This isn't a good place." Vash frowned as she leaned over the seat. "The magic was warped and dark."

Harris frowned as he nodded. "I agree. But there hasn't been magic here in a long time."

Vash shook her head and a couple of faded sparks fell toward my leg. A couple of months of practice stopped my reflex to brush them off before they faded into nothing. "It used to be a portal, but nothing comes through now. A great battle closed it. We shouldn't be here."

"She's right." Harris made a circular motion for me to turn around and leave. "I don't even want to get out of the car. Now that we know about it, maybe I can get the coven up here someday and clean it up. It's definitely daylight work. I wouldn't want to be here in the night."

"I could help with that." Vash sank back in her seat and hugged herself.

"We'll see about that." I headed back down the road. It was one thing to have Vash out trying to help Harris find the source of strange magic, but something totally different for her to be dealing with dark magic that left trees twisted and the whole area feeling dark and deadly.

The dark dead-end had hit Vash so hard that she didn't even look up as we passed the camel. She sat in the back seat with her arms around herself and her eyes closed. Even though I didn't have her magical senses, I knew she was disturbed by what we'd stumbled on. If it was anything that might come after her, I was ready to meet it with fangs, claws, and magical bullets.

7

"Turn left up here." Harris pointed as we headed toward the next spot that felt odd to him. He frowned slightly.

"What's wrong?" I steered through the turn he'd indicated, and we were pointing east, heading back toward the interstate.

"I've never felt anything like this in the area, but then I'm not usually out here this time of year." Harris tapped the dashboard.

"Okay, what's out here?" The whole area looked like a cross between upscale homes on large plots of land, and farm/ranchland that had been in families for generations.

"The renaissance faire." Harris pursed his lips. "The magic seems to be coming from that direction."

Vash leaned between the seats and pointed to a butte rising above the trees. "It's over there."

"Right." Harris nodded. "And the faire site is at the bottom of that hill."

The high-rising landmark looked more like a butte than a hill to me. From what I could tell, it had a flat top and was more of a rock formation than the foothills we'd been driving in.

"Is this going to be a problem?" The way the day was going, there was a good chance for a problem.

"Maybe, maybe not." Harris scratched his short blond beard. "We're going to proceed like it won't be."

I didn't like the way that sounded but opted to not press things. "Okay, just tell me where to park."

Harris continued scratching. "Parking. Hmmm…are we up for a short hike?"

We drove past a locked gate that would've opened onto a huge grassy parking lot. On the far side of the opening was something that looked like a wooden façade of a castle wall. Overall, the place had a fairly rundown feel to it.

"Yeah, that's the way it's coming from." Harris looked out the window. "Never felt it before, but then maybe I wouldn't. There's always been lots of people here when I've been here in the past. That would've muffled the feeling of magic."

I let the brief description go. It made a little sense to me and I wasn't ready for Harris to drop into lecture mode. If magical senses worked like physical ones, I could see where lots of people would make it hard to pick up on something, even if it was out of the ordinary.

"It's very strong." Vash stayed leaning between us, and I wished she'd stop it. Just because she could survive a crash didn't mean she wouldn't draw attention, and I really didn't want to get pulled over.

"Turn left again, into this next drive." Harris pointed again. "I think we can park up here and not attract too much attention."

It was the dirt drive of a small church hidden in the trees along the side of the hill that rolled up toward the north. I went as he instructed and we found ourselves in a parking lot that was nearly surrounded by thick trees. Someone just driving past wouldn't see the car, but anyone coming into the lot would.

"We're not too far from the site." Harris undid his seat belt.

Vash frowned as she got out of the car and looked toward the butte. "It calls to me. Why is that? Could Djinn magic have made it?"

"That's possible." Harris came around to stand next to her.

"Then you'll give me a moment to get ready." At the last site, we hadn't gotten out of the car. There had been an implied safety in that. I opened the hatch of the Outback and pulled out my big magic sword.

Garnet and the others had been helping me learn to use it. She was part of a reenactment group, so she was good with weapons like swords and axes. I still didn't want to go up against a master swordsman, but I could at least strike a blow now and again. I strapped the sword on, knowing it would vanish from casual sight. Then I grabbed a couple of extra magazines for Stormbringer, my magical handgun. Since I didn't know exactly what I was going to need, I also shoved in a few extra bullets. There was no way I was heading toward something that was pulling at Vash without being armed to the teeth.

Harris frowned at me as he took the backpack

he'd brought along out of the cargo area next to my sword. "We're going to be cutting across a deserted faire site, do you really think all that is necessary?"

I pulled out the staff Harris had put in, in case he needed a focus, and tossed it to him. "Yeah, something's pulling at Vash, we're going to be ready for anything."

"Okay, fine." Harris caught the staff and tapped it a couple of times on the ground. "You might be right. Whatever is in these strange feelings, this one is stronger than the last one."

"And the last one had twisted the trees around it." I closed the back of the car and clicked the key fob to lock it. "Yeah, I'm ready for this one."

It didn't take us long to reach the nearest gate that led into the vast parking lot that, if it had been paved, would've put some dying malls to shame. The place looked like it could use a fleet of trucks with dirt road base to fill in the ruts and gullies that covered the place. I'd honestly been on roads in third world countries that looked smoother than the parking area did.

"Let's stay near the trees." I wasn't sure I liked the idea of walking out in the open. Something about the area had my wolf near to the surface, on guard.

"It'll take longer." Harris pointed across the parking lot.

"Amuse me. I didn't know we were on a schedule here." I took Vash's hand. Maybe if I kept her close at hand, I'd feel better about her safety. If Harris hadn't done so much for us, I wouldn't have put her in potential danger to help him out without something that was just a bad feeling.

"No schedule," Harris muttered as we skirted a corral and headed into a shorter, newer forest than the one near the church.

"Good." I glanced around at the place that felt like there hadn't been any people around for a few months. "Are we trespassing?"

Harris shrugged. "Technically. If we get in trouble, I'll call Briar and he'll work it out. As one of his local magical contacts, I get a bit of leeway when it comes to things like this *if* I can prove it's magic-related."

"And if we can't prove that?"

"Then we go to court. Luckily, I've got friends who know Jamie Eden, the guy who owns this place. We'll work it out." Harris pressed on.

The answer wasn't the best in the world. I hated the idea of calling Agent Briar of the shadowy FBI group that oversaw the supernatural community. Sure, he'd helped me adjust to being a werewolf, after pulling me out of Afghanistan, but he was probably way too busy to get involved in something like getting us out of a trespassing charge. And, just because he knew someone who knew the owner didn't mean they could negotiate something to get us out of trouble. The situation was getting worse by the moment.

A vacant single-wide trailer hid behind another line of low trees.

There was something there. I didn't know what, but it was hard to not tighten my hand on Vash's. Holding her closer wasn't going to keep her safe if something started happening. A rough track meandered through the slowly thickening forest. The first spot that was an obvious campsite came into view and my nerves grew tighter. Like the ruts in the parking lot, it made me flash back to Afghanistan and some of the insurgent camps we'd come across. I doubted the people who camped there were preparing for war, but the feeling hit me and I didn't like it.

"Where are we going?" I stared at Harris' back.

He gestured to the south with his staff. "I'd say at the base of the hill."

"He's right." Vash tugged my hand. "It might be Fae magic, but I can't be sure. I've only met a couple of them over the years. You can relax, Lucas, if it is Fae, they won't mean us harm."

I shook my head. "Sorry, Vash, I'll relax when we're back in the car and driving away from here." My vision sharpened as my wolf pushed a little more out from the depths of my soul and peered out, trying to give me another edge to help keep Vash safe.

"You might be right, Vash." Harris paced at my side. "Sorry, I'm a little distracted. I've never been back here before. I knew some of the faire folk lived back here during the faire, but it's kinda cool being back here."

"Looks like a terrorist camp to me."

Harris stopped and stared around. "I guess it might. Lucas, you're good at ruining a mood."

I laughed but didn't feel joyous. "That's me. Mood Ruiner. Now let's find this spot, see what's going on, and get out of here."

A few wooden buildings appeared and disappeared in the trees as we hiked along. Some of the campsites had been better cleaned out than others, and they all looked like it had been fairly recently that they'd been occupied. No rain or wind had disturbed the tire tracks where cars and trucks had rolled across the rough roads.

"That way." Harris pointed his staff to the right. "We're getting close."

Vash nodded but didn't say anything. She still had her hand in mine, and she seemed to vibrate with extra energy like she was about to explode.

By the time Harris called us to a stop, the strange energy was so thick, the hair on my arms stood out, and my wolf had set up a long, drawn-out growl.

"Definitely an Underhill gate." Harris stood facing a rock wall that formed the base of the butte.

"And something's come through recently." Vash looked around like she was expecting something to rush out at us.

I fought the urge to pick her up. If I had her in my arms, I wouldn't be able to draw Stormbringer or my sword.

"Let me see if I can figure out how to track down whatever it was." Harris took off the pack he'd grabbed out of the Outback and dug into it. "Luckily, I brought a few things to help with that."

He held up a stone on a string. "Let's start easy."

Vash looked at him. "I haven't seen a pendulum for a long time. There are easier ways."

"Like what?" Harris cocked an eyebrow.

After looking up at me as if for permission, Vash smiled. "Let's see what the winds of time have to show us."

She spread her hands wide and smoke filled the space between them. Closing her eyes, she started muttering something that reminded me of some of the Arabic dialects I'd heard, possibly Pashto. A scene, almost like a hologram solidified in the smoke.

At first, it looked like sparks flew from the forest and into a soft glow against the wall of the butte.

"Can you slow it down a little, Vash?" Harris walked around her, staring intensely at the scene.

She didn't open her eyes, but the sparks stopped moving so quickly and little figures emerged in the center of the glows. They looked like tiny, misshapen, miss-colored people with insect wings.

I caught my breath. She was showing us fairies. I never actually seen fairies.

"They're running from something." Harris walked around Vash's smoking hands as if he might be able to see something different from another angle.

"What do fairies run from?" With people, I could understand things they would run from, but if fairies were magical creatures, the only thing they should be afraid of was something bigger and more powerful than they were. I wasn't sure if I wanted to encounter something that would scare fairies, particularly not with Vash in tow.

"They aren't as powerful as you might think," Harris stepped back. "Vash, can you expand your scene? We need more information."

The smoky hologram shifted, swinging around

as Vash wiggled her fingers like she was turning a globe.

"Stop." Harris pointed at the larger figure that appeared.

A tall, elegant figure with dark hair and skin stood near the tree I was in front of. I turned and glanced at the tree to make sure the cloaked figure wasn't still there.

"A Dark Elf," Harris muttered. "There was a Dark Elf here in Colorado?"

Vash shook out her hands and the scene vanished. "And it was hunting the smaller Fae. That's wrong."

"Why is it wrong?" I looked at the wall of the butte, there wasn't any evidence of the portal the small Fae had been escaping through.

Harris hummed. "I don't know tons about Fae politics, or pecking order, or whatever you want to call it, but as I understand it, the larger Fae don't consider their much smaller cousins as a threat, so they don't normally attack anyone unless they're the same size or larger."

I still didn't get it. "So what if the little ones took the fight to the bigger one?"

"They're small, not stupid." Harris put his hand on the wall where the portal had been. "I can't tell if the Dark Elf made it through the portal."

Vash's breath caught and she dashed to a bush near the rocks. "This is bad." She picked up a large butterfly, then turned it over in her hands. A tiny misshapen body was attached to the golden-edged black wings. Its skin was dark, somewhere between brown and black.

Harris stared. "Fae disappear from this world when they're killed."

"This is bad," Vash repeated.

"And it means what?" I resisted the urge to reach forward and move the unmoving tiny hands that looked like they only had three fingers and not fully formed arms. They were missing joints, bones, or something. I couldn't exactly identify it.

"We need to get it back to Faerie." Harris went back to his pack. "Vash, do you think you can help me open the portal again?"

A tear streamed down her face as she looked up at the stony face of the butte. "Together. Yes. The portal calls to me, but I'm not strong enough."

"Do we need more people?" I hated going into the unknown without a full unit around me. It might take us a couple of hours to get everyone there, but it might be worth it, might mean the difference between success and failure.

Harris took out a piece of chalk and shook his head. "No time. This little fairy needs to go back to its land of origin now." He started making marks on the stone.

Comparing what he did to where the portal had been in Vash's smoky hologram, it looked like he'd outlined the portal.

"Hold on to her, Lucas." Vash thrust her hands toward me with the little fairy there waiting for me to take.

It was small enough to fill one of my large hands. The wings were soft like those of a butterfly, and the body was so light I almost didn't feel it lying there. I wasn't sure what I should do as Vash and

Harris worked their magic.

Harris traced a circle with his staff, then Vash stepped up and repeated the motion with her hand. She had to float up slightly to get to the top of the circle. Where her hand passed, a glowing line of power danced across the rocks.

"Good," Harris muttered. He spun his staff twice, then tapped the small symbols he'd drawn on the rocks.

"No." Vash shook her head. "That's the wrong order. It feels wrong." She floated over to the rocks and tapped the symbols slightly differently than Harris had done.

The line of power Vash had created spun clockwise and slowly the energy filled in the gap like a whirlpool in a small lake. The energy blazed yellow and green. It grew so bright, I had to turn away, as a warm breeze rushed out away from the butte.

I turned back.

The portal stood open. Something shimmered beyond the edge of energy.

A swarm of tiny Fae shot out of the portal, their shouts raised so high I had to drop the little fairy I held to slam my hands over my ears.

8

They surged out of the portal like a swarm of hornets pouring out of a nest that had been knocked to the ground. Their high-pitched battle cries were painful, and I hadn't thought to bring any earplugs. A storm of bright and dark wings rushed us.

"Get back." I grabbed Vash's hand and stumbled a few steps away from the butte.

Something slashed into my neck. Pain lashed through me. I slapped at my neck and my hand brushed wings. "They've got swords, knives, something."

Harris spun his staff. "Working on it."

Vash spread her free hand. "Stop. We're friendly."

Her words didn't seem to have any effect. More of the small Fae gushed out of the portal.

I yanked Stormbringer free of its holster and fired toward the magical gateway they were coming from. Fire spun from the bullet as it flew through the air, then exploded as it encountered the magic powering the portal.

"Lucas, don't do that." Harris batted some of the Sprites with his staff. "Portals aren't always stable, your magic bullets might cause it to explode, or close."

"Not sure that would be bad." I backhanded one of the diminutive attackers hard enough to throw it back through the portal. If we could close the portal, it would at least stop the flow of the little buggers.

Vash shook her head as smoky magic flowed out of her and collided with the portal's power. "They're keeping it open. I can't close it."

"That's bad." I holstered my sidearm and yanked the sword free of its scabbard. Maybe the more limited reach would be safer. As I started hitting the Sprites out the air, I vowed I wasn't going to name the sword Faeswatter…no way.

Harris was knocking little Fae into the surrounding trees and rocks with his staff.

I turned my blade so I was using the flat. It slowed movement down a bit but gave me a greater surface to catch the bugs with. It felt like for every Sprite I knocked out of the air, three more took its place. The portal continued to pulse and spin and the air around me got more and more crowded with every second.

The Sprites dashed in and out of reach faster than I could really follow. Each one seemed to strike skin with their tiny weapons. Some left thorn-like darts in my hands and arms, others slashed at my neck and face. It was worse than being outside in a sandstorm.

I growled, my wolf wanting to come out and lay waste to them. Each wound was like another tick biting into us. I didn't want to lose it and potentially hurt Vash or Harris. I let him out just enough to increase my speed and endurance as I turned my sword into a dangerous fan of Fae death.

Dust and bits of wings covered the flat of my sword, and I didn't have anything real to show for my efforts. I wished Stormbringer was a larger weapon, with a huge magazine so I could just shout for Vash and Harris to get down while I filled the air with lead. I'd always preferred precision to just spraying, but sometimes, the situation called for suppressing fire that wasn't perfectly aimed, and fighting a bunch of tiny Fae spilling out of a magical portal was one of those situations.

Then, as suddenly as they started, the assault stopped. The tiny slashes on my exposed skin ended.

Vash stood in front of me with her arms spread, wisps of smoke flowed from her hands as red sparks cascaded in an almost constant flow from her hair. A glowing bubble of magic stood between us and the little Fae, some of which had smashed into it. A cloud of Fae flew around the barrier, buzzing like pissed off bees.

"I can't hold them off long." Vash shook from the effort.

"Can you teleport us out of here?" Harris crouched low, with his staff ready to go some more, but sweat matted his long blond hair to his scalp and his breath was coming out in ragged gasps. He wasn't up for much more.

Vash shook her head. "Not and hold them off. If I move us with them around us, they can follow."

I'd never heard of Fae teleporting but didn't really want to be getting Fae guts off the windshield of the Outback. "Harris, we need ideas."

He wiped wet hair out of his eyes. "You could

go wolf and get Vash out of here. Get help and come back for me."

"Nope." I shook my head and took a couple of deep breaths. Sometimes getting air when I could was important. "Not leaving you behind. How do we close the portal?"

"Disrupt the runes." He pointed out the marks he and Vash had made. "Should bring it down."

I pulled out Stormbringer. "That I can do."

Harris straightened and touched my arm. "We don't know what that will do with the anchoring energy of the portal."

Glancing at the swarming Fae, I shook my head. "If it takes them out, so be it." I touched Vash's shoulder. "Get behind me." I wasn't sure how much I could shield her if things started exploding, but I was a werewolf. According to everyone around me, that meant fairly indestructible unless there was silver, magic, or fangs involved. We were able to find out how portal magic fit into that.

I popped out the magazine of magical bullets I'd been using and put in some basic regular old rounds I'd bought at the sporting goods store. All I needed to do was disrupt the runes, I hoped that meant change them. I focused on the first glowing symbol and squeezed off a round.

The magic didn't seem to affect the lead as it flew through the swirling glow. It impacted the rock of the butte right where the rune glowed. Sparks flew. Chips of stone exploded from the strike and the rune stopped glowing.

A ripple of red ran through the portal.

The Fae screamed louder. It would've been so

nice to have ear plugs or some other hearing protection.

"Hit the next one," Harris urged. "This might actually work."

Vash touched my leg. "Lucas, hurry." Her voice was barely loud enough to pick up through the screaming Fae who were pounding against her protective barrier.

I wanted to scoop her up and run. When her barrier came down we were going to be covered in Sprites. There was nothing I could do about that, except cut off their flow.

"Get ready." Since the first shot had an effect, I focused on the second and third runes so I could get off two shots before turning my sights on the ones along the bottom of the portal.

With each shot, the portal shimmered again, sending more red through the swirls of color. I hoped that meant it was destabilizing. I kept my fingers crossed as I retargeted and got off another round.

The red spread wasn't as vast, then yellows and oranges burst out of the portal, like something on the other side was trying to get out.

Something glowed next to the runes I'd defaced.

"Someone's trying to stabilize it." Harris straightened and pounded the butt of his staff on the ground.

"Who?" I went ahead and shot the final rune even as a new glowing symbol appeared next to it.

The portal swirled faster, but the flow of Fae had stopped, or at least I thought it had. The swarming Sprites became harder to see through.

Then something human-sized stepped through, followed by two more. From what I could tell, they were in bright-colored armor and had swords at their sides.

"Shit. Elves." Harris muttered.

"I'm sorry, Lucas." Vash's voice faded off.

I spun toward Vash in time to see her turn to a puff of smoke and flow into my pocket, where her bell was. She'd pushed herself to her limit and was out of the game. The barrier disappeared as the sound of a sword coming free of its scabbard rang through the forest. The sudden silence of the Sprites was deafening.

9

The Sprites flew in a tight tornadic formation around us just a couple of feet from us, closer than Vash's shield had let them come.

"This isn't good." Harris tightened his hands on his staff. "I hate dealing with Elves."

"Done it very often?" I wasn't sure what my best bet was going to be, Stormbringer or the sword. The Elves were human-sized and thus easier targets than the smaller Sprites, but something told me they were probably good at dodging. But I was better with the handgun. I sheathed the sword and pulled it out.

"No, thank the gods." Harris spread his feet, and defensively held his staff across his body, ready for whatever was going to come next.

Although I worried about Vash overextending herself again, I couldn't stop and pull out her bell and cradle it, willing a bit of my personal energy to her until she was strong enough to be solid again. We'd never actually tried that, but Harris and Cin Kilkari thought it might work.

"What do we do?" Holding Stormbringer made me feel a little more in control.

"I can't match them magically." Harris's voice

was barely a whisper, and before I'd become a werewolf, I wouldn't have caught his words. "Let's see if we can talk our way out of this."

Diplomacy wasn't my strong point. Army Rangers went in when diplomacy had failed. I'd spent years being the muscle. "Then you do the talking."

The circling wall of Sprites separated, with the diminutive Fae flying up and over the opening they created to let the Elves get closer to us.

There was no denying that the Elves were pretty. Their beauty was stunning. On a pageant runway, they would've stunned everyone there with their elegant grace and appearance. Even their armor and swords were crafted to enhance their innate loveliness.

"Where is the Djinn?" With perfect English, the closest one glared from me to Harris.

I glanced at Harris.

"Don't try to hide her. We felt her magic open the portal." The Elf rested a hand on the hilt of his sweeping, elegant sword.

"The Djinn is of no importance." Harris tapped his staff on the ground. "I'm the local guardian here. Why have you created a portal without my permission?"

"Djinn are always important." The Elves turned their attention on Harris. "This portal has been here for many years. We have an agreement with the owner of this land to have it so that our people may have easy access to the celebration that is held on these grounds."

Celebration? I looked at Harris, wondering if

they were talking about the renefaire, or something else.

Harris squared his shoulders and glared. It was the best tough-guy act I'd ever seen him put on. When it came to magical things, he took his job of high priest seriously. "But you haven't contacted the proper magical authorities to have a portal here."

The Elves glanced at each other as the Sprites continued to whirl around us.

Frowning, the one who'd been talking glared back at Harris. "Rulers of the Fae don't need human permission to create portals to your world."

"That's not how it is anymore." Harris matched his glare. "Are either one of you a member of the high court?"

The question elicited an indignant huff. "Like a member of the high court would foul themselves with coming to this magicless mud-ball."

Harris smiled slightly and leaned on his staff, looking like he thought he'd managed to get the upper hand. "Yet, you came in response to us opening the portal. We had found a dead Sprite and were trying to return it to your realm before a non-mage stumbled across it. Something killed one of yours."

I wanted to target one of the two Elves but didn't want to make the tense situation worse. With luck, I could hit them before they hit us but needed to give Harris a chance to do his thing. From the past times Vash had overextended herself, I knew she was going to be out for a little while. If the Elves were looking for her, I hoped she'd be out until we could at least get back to the car.

Again, the Elf huffed. "Sprites are Fae, but they aren't Elves. Don't insult us, human."

"Regardless, something killed it, and it didn't return to your realm when it died." Harris kept his voice level and fairly passive. "From what we could discover, a Dark Elf killed it."

The two Elves looked at each other again. The one who'd been doing all the talking then gestured and one of the Sprites, a larger one with glowing green wings, came down to him…at least I was fairly sure the Elf was male. The Sprite landed on his hand for a moment. Something passed between the two that sounded like bird song, then the Sprite lifted up and flew toward the base of the butte where the portal had been. With the faintest of flashes, the Sprite vanished through the portal that had faded from view when the Elves arrived.

"Dark Elves are a concern of ours." The Elf turned back to Harris. "But that need not concern you, human." He looked around and his gaze settled on where I'd dropped the dead Sprite. Without saying anything, he pointed toward it and the other one walked out of the wall of Sprites over to it.

Deep inside, my wolf growled. This talking went against his nature too. We were both creatures of action. I pushed him back, willing him to stay down, but be ready if the situation changed.

The Elf turned his attention to me for the first time. His gaze stabbed through me, feeling like he knew everything in a moment of study before looking back at Harris. "Your wolf is on edge. It is best that we conclude this soon. Tell him to hand over the Djinn and we will leave you both in peace."

It was Harris's turn to huff. "He's not my wolf. He's the rightful bearer of the Djinn's vessel."

"Then we shall kill him to free the Djinn of his influence." The Elf tightened his hand on his sword's pommel. "Djinn must be neutralized."

My grip on Stormbringer reflexively tightened as I brought the pistol up. "This Djinn isn't going to be neutralized."

Harris touched my hand. "Relax, Lucas, I've got this."

I hoped he was right. Without moving, I gave him the briefest nod. Odds were, I wasn't going to like where the idea of neutralizing Vash went. She'd spent two thousand years lost in the desert, trapped in the confines of her bell. There was no way I was going to let something like that, or worse happen to her again.

"We need to know why it's important that the Djinn be neutralized." Harris leveled his gaze at the Elf. "She is nothing to you."

"You know very little of what is important to Elves." The Elf looked like he was going to say something else when the other one came back through the wall of Sprites. He stopped and they exchanged a quick sing-song series of comments.

With a frown, the Elf turned his attention back on us. "Your assessment of the situation with the death of the Sprite is correct. We must go. Turn over the Djinn's vessel."

Harris tightened his grip on his staff as my hands flexed with my need to shoot the asshole.

"No." Power rolled off Harris, and I wondered what he was about to do.

If he attacked, I was ready to fill the two Elves with lead. It took all my control to not fire the first shot. Deep inside me, my wolf was ready to do just that, and follow it up with fangs and claws, if need be.

"Take us to the Fae Court and let them make the case, and hear us out," Harris demanded. "We won't turn the vessel over to anyone but your king or queen." His staff started glowing softly.

"We could just take the vessel from your corpses." The Elf glared back but moved his hand from his sword. "But perhaps this is what it needs to be. A war with the humans wouldn't benefit us at this time."

With a wide wave of his hand, the Elf poured magic toward the portal. He didn't need to create the runes Harris and Vash had used. The portal sprung to life and he and the other Elf strode toward the swirling vortex of power. Without any perceivable order from the Elf, the Sprites changed their flight pattern. They still kept us surrounded in a wall of wings and tiny swords, but they formed a tunnel that extended to the edge of the portal.

Harris glanced at me. "Ready for a trip to Faerie?"

There were so many more things that I thought might be safer things to do with our day. I worried we might be taking Vash into danger. She would be safer far away from there. Would we be able to fight our way out of there? Would we be trapped forever, or worse? The intel wasn't complete. I hated not having all the intel.

The silent Elf stepped to the side as we reached

the portal. He waved us on. "Please go first."

I shook my head but doubted he was going to go first. "How about we go together?"

"We don't trust each other. I can respect that, wolf." He bowed slightly.

Harris vanished, following the Elf who'd handled most of the negotiating.

With a deep breath to steady myself as my pulse raced faster and faster, I stepped through the portal. The magic swept around me. It was totally different from when Vash used her power to teleport us. I felt like a leaf caught in a strong stream. Everything spun first one direction then another. The magic danced like a live wire. Deep inside my wolf whined, and I hoped the disorientation would end quickly.

10

About the time my stomach was ready to revolt as the spinning magic tossed me every way possible, everything eased and quieted. Light blazed around us and we stepped out onto a rocky cliffside. The uneven cliffs stretched as far as I could see. At the bottom, many hundreds of feet below, jagged rocks waited for anyone unlucky enough to fall, or jump to their deaths.

"Not what I expected a fairyland to look like." I glanced around.

The Sprites weren't with us, and I wondered where they might be, but didn't want to sound stupid asking a question that might be obvious to the others. If the portal was anything like Vash's teleporting, we might've gone wherever our Elven guards wanted to take us, and the Sprites might've wanted to go somewhere else and got off the magical express way at a different exit.

The sky was dark and felt dangerous. The flatness seemed to hide storms that waited for the right moment to lash out and destroy us. There was just enough space on the endless rocky trail for two people to walk side by side. Looking up the stone wall, it was taller than any mountain I'd ever seen.

The rough surface disappeared into the depressing sky with no signs of stopping. It made me wonder if that was what it was like to look toward Everest when you were hiking along one of the trails near the base of the tallest mountain on Earth.

"Faerie is a mix of landscapes." Harris also looked about as if he was more than a little surprised at where we found ourselves.

"You've been here before?" Like most of my new friends, I seemed to be constantly learning new things about Harris.

He shook his head. "Not exactly here, but I've been through portals before. Normally just a few steps beyond the event horizon."

Another new term. "That's what the edge of a portal is called? Like a black hole?"

"Sounds appropriate, doesn't it?"

"Yeah, I guess it does." A soft flapping noise drew my attention.

The Elf in front of us stopped and stared up the stony wall. "Against the rocks and stay still." He pressed himself tight, smoothing his sword down so it didn't point out, making an obvious target.

Whatever else he might be, he was clearly a warrior.

I copied his move. The rocks pushed my sword into my back, but I tried to ignore it and look like nothing more than a lump there on the side of the mountain trail.

Beside me, Harris tucked himself in, holding his staff at his side.

Something light gray separated from the sky and swooped towards us. I knew better than to turn my head. The least little movement could give our position away. Contrary to belief, it wasn't color that revealed something trying to hide, it was movement. A soldier in a bright red suit could stand perfectly still in a field near a tree line and as long as he wasn't moving, most people wouldn't see him. Now if he moved while people were looking his direction, the odds were he'd be spotted. Pressed there against the rock wall with some unknown beast flying toward us, I really wanted more cover and hoped we were all being still enough to avoid detection. If it relied on something like heat vision, or anything more sensitive than the basic visual spectrum, we were so screwed.

My eyes hurt from me trying to see more details, but I kept my head still and hoped if it attacked, we'd have the seconds needed for me to bring Stormbringer to bear and get some shots off.

Pale gray wings snapped open wider than some combat jets.

It had to be a Dragon. That was the only thing it could be. My breath caught. I hadn't even been in Faerie for fifteen minutes and I was already seeing my first Dragon. It bent its reptilian head toward the trail and soared out over the edge where it dropped off to the treacherous rocks. Its scales were shiny silver more than soft gray, but in the treacherous light they didn't reflect much. It was longer than a fighter jet, and no doubt just as deadly.

When it vanished below the trail, I released the breath I'd held longer than I had realized. My head spun a little as oxygen rushed back to my brain. Other than breathing, I did my best to not move until given the all-clear by our Elf guide, captor, I wasn't sure what our standing was.

"Stay." The Elf next to me made the slightest gesture as another of the beasts came down from the dark clouds.

Like the first one, it was pale silver as it sliced through the air, sweeping lower toward the trail. Its heavy wingbeats thrummed through me, vibrating along the sword on my back and it was all I could do to not shiver.

It was nearly past, when Harris shifted and his staff clattered to the stones of the trail.

The Dragon snaked its head toward us as its body kept flying through the air above the trail. The scales around its opalescent eyes moved, widening like a camera iris.

"Run." The lead Elf jerked away from the wall and dashed down the trail.

Not needing to be told twice, I followed him, pulling Stormbringer out as we went. There was no way I was going to try to face a Dragon with something as useless as a sword. If there was one thing I wasn't, it was a knight of old.

Harris snatched up his staff and was just a couple of feet behind me. "Two freaking Dragons."

"I'd rather just watch from a distance." Deep inside me, the wolf uncurled, lending me his stamina to keep up with the Elf.

"We're almost there." The Elf barely glanced over his shoulder to make sure we were still there.

I wondered where 'there' was.

The Elf following Harris shouted something right before a Dragon roared.

Things got hot.

A blast of fire flowed past us and left scorch marks on the trail before cascading over the edge.

"Cover me." The leading Elf, the one who'd done most of the talking back on Earth, faced the wall and began working magic.

Hoping regular bullets might have an impact, I turned and aimed at the Dragon who was flapping its wings like some kind of giant hummingbird as it breathed fire at the other Elf who'd crafted a magical shield to hold back the flames. With any luck, a shield that held back fire wouldn't stop bullets from flying from the inside of it. Focusing on the strangely-opening-and-closing eye closest to me, I squeezed off two rounds and held my breath.

Stormbringer's thunder rolled across the trail.

The Dragon jerked away. Something pale sprayed from its head.

It roared.

Harris waved his staff and a fresh shield erupted between me and the fount of flame that nearly hit me as the Dragon retaliated.

Hoping I had the right magazine, I frantically switched ordinance. If the regular bullet had caused a real reaction, maybe a magical one would make a bigger impact. In a regular fight, I knew what it would take to bring down an opponent. I'd never faced a Dragon before.

"Wait for me to drop the shield," Harris's voice sounded strained.

I targeted the Dragon's head again and waited.

The Dragon must've run out of breath after a couple of minutes. The flames stopped and it inhaled.

Harris dropped the shield and I fired.

With the magical bullet, Stormbringer's roar was a lot louder. It blazed from the gun barrel, leaving a trail of fire. The impact with the Dragon was a lot more fantastic. A ball of fire engulfed the beast's head. It coughed. A return jet of flames didn't happen.

I fired again, for good measure.

A roar of fury came from down the trail.

The first Dragon was coming back.

Magical light illuminated the dark metal of my pistol's barrel. I turned toward the portal that glowed on the stone wall.

"Hurry." The Elf looked a little shaky as he stepped through the passage without waiting for us to follow.

"Harris, move." I waved Stormbringer toward the portal. "I'll hold it off if I have to." My magical bullets were working. The second Dragon wasn't down, but it was limping away. Part of me wanted to finish it off, but I had no idea how intelligent they were. Did they have Dragon doctors, or something similar? Did it have a way to survive the damage I'd done or was it just going to fly away and wait for the end to come? Part of me hated not knowing, not being able to do the right thing. Then the other Dragon blasted flame at us.

The Elf guarding our rear turned and cast a shield just in time.

Harris went through the portal.

"Go, human." The Elf forced the words out through gritted teeth. His words were strangely accented with no little amount of hate.

I squeezed off two shots in tight formation, aiming at the heart of the flames spewing toward us. Regular ammo would've melted before reaching the Dragon's mouth, hopefully, Urson's magic bullets would be fire resistant until they released their own blast. Not waiting to see if I had hit something, I dashed for the portal and dove through, hoping I'd be landing on something softer than the rocks we'd been walking along.

When things work right, it's always awesome. The grass on the other side of the portal cushioned my landing and I managed to roll out of the way before the Elf behind me rushed through, flames erupting around him.

As I got to my feet, coming up in a crouch with Stormbringer pointed at the portal, the lead Elf gestured and shouted something in their singsong language. The portal flashed and fell in on itself.

With a deep breath, I lowered my sidearm and glanced at Harris who was standing a few feet away with his staff pointed toward the spot where the portal had been moments before.

The rear Elf stomped over to the one who'd just closed the portal and shouted something to him, pointing angrily back at the place we'd stepped into the much greener space.

Voice raised to meet his compatriot, the other chattered something in reply before turning away and stomping off across the verdant meadow we found ourselves in.

Harris shrugged when I glanced at him questioningly. I hoped he might speak whatever tongue they were using, but he looked as confused as I was. Something big had happened, maybe bigger than the Dragons that had just attacked us. I wanted to know what it was.

"Hey, what's going on?" I hurried after the Elf who was leading us through this strange adventure.

"Don't worry about it, wolf." He didn't even turn toward me, just kept marching along angrily. "It's none of your concern."

I grabbed his shoulder and spun him around. "Wrong. It is my concern. My friend and I nearly died back there when those Dragons attacked. You and your buddy seem to be worried about the Dragons, so tell me what's up. If it happens again, we might be more help."

The Elf squinted at me. His green eyes were harsh, like a thorn bush waiting to scratch at the least little opportunity. After a moment, he let out a breath. "Those Dragons shouldn't have been there. I'm trying to pick a course that will be easy enough for you and the human."

He sounded like he knew where we were going and had particular things in mind. I didn't doubt that he was trying to hide things from us. If our circumstances had been reversed, I would've done the same thing, particularly if the regular trip would've taken unknown people through sensitive areas. But there was so much he wasn't telling me, and I was beginning to wonder what we'd managed to step in. Was it tied to a dead Sprite on Earth, or something bigger and more dangerous?

I stopped myself from touching the pocket where Vash's bell was. How long would she have to stay there before she was strong enough to return to our world? Would it be long enough that Harris and I could get back to Earth? Or would she emerge into the troubling Fae worlds we'd fallen into?

Something behind us roared.

Bringing Stormbringer back up, I searched the rolling green for signs of anything dangerous.

The Elf muttered something that sounded like a curse.

"Run, wolf. Run for everything you're worth." He turned and dashed off the direction we'd been going.

"Harris, run!" I waved Stormbringer high and took out after the Elf. I didn't like running from anything but figured if the Elf was making a break for it, we probably should too.

More roars and snarls erupted on our trail as we sprinted across the short grass meadow. There was nowhere to hide. I could only hope that over the next rise, or down the next valley there might be some rocks, a cave, or something. At that point, another portal would even be a good idea.

The ground shook as we started down a valley. Someone shouted. I glanced behind us. My first thought was Native Americans in old western movies, but they weren't mounted on horses, they were huge cat-like creatures. The riders, huge green brutes that looked more like gorillas than men, didn't carry bows and arrows but long spears.

We were massively outnumbered. I hoped the

Elf a few feet ahead of me was going to be able to pull a portal out of his ass or something that would keep us safe. The more magic I was exposed to, the less I liked it. I wished I could go back to boring, sand-filled patrols in the Afghan desert.

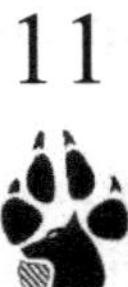

The Elf skidded to a stop next to a small bush.

"They're way too close." I forced out as my body complained about the running from the gorilla things riding huge cats.

"Patience, Wolf." The Elf tore at the bush, tossing branches and leaves out of the way. The way it moved, he didn't appear to be tearing apart a living bush but removing twigs put over a hole, or something.

The Elf bringing up the rear shouted something in their language.

I was getting way tired of not being able to understand what was going on. I doubted I could do much to help the Elf with his bush problem. I turned toward the oncoming riders. If there was something I was good at, it was shooting things.

As I squeezed the trigger, Stormbringer roared louder than the cat and gorillas combined. Maybe, if I took out a few of them, it would give the others something to think about. My first short blazed across the meadow and caught one of the gorillas in the chest. The bullet's fire exploded and knocked him from his mount, but he somehow landed on his feet. The magical fire danced across his armor like some kind of special effect before it died away. He threw his head back and yelled something that sounded like a battle cry.

"Fireball bullets aren't helping," I muttered as I frantically switched magazines. Maybe lightning would have a better effect on them.

"Orcs are resistant to most magic." Harris stopped beside me, panting for breath.

I squeezed off another shot at the same Orc, aiming for its head.

It brought up a huge shield and deflected the bullet, sending it flying off into the sky where the lightning danced about before dying.

"Okay. No magic." I popped the lightning magazine.

"This way." The rear Elf pointed toward the other one, who'd finished uncovering a hole that lead into darkness.

"Better be a safe spot." I jammed the lighting rounds back into the gun and ran toward the hole, following the lead Elf as he slid down something that resembled a pipe leading deep into the earth.

The pipe slide wound us down toward a glowing, spinning, blue maw. The Elf ahead of me didn't appear worried, so I did my best to slow my beating heart as we bounced along. He disappeared in a vibrant azure blast. I was seconds behind him.

Having been through a couple of portals already, this one wasn't nearly as disorienting as the first one. My feet hit soft ground and I bent my knees to roll a short distance away. I came up in a crouch and leveled Stormbringer at the exit portal that rotated the opposite way the entrance had and was a softer shade of blue.

Lead Elf was just a few feet from me as Harris came through the portal a lot less gracefully than I had. Rear Elf made his exit, landing on his feet like he took magical slides all the time, and for what I knew, he might have just done that.

Shouting something in their tongue, Lead Elf thrust his hands toward the portal and magic met magic, shutting down the passage that had been our escape. I wondered if the Orcs had followed us down the hole if they were now on the other side of the portal trying to figure out how they were going to get back up the slide and out to safety.

I lowered Stormbringer and looked around. We were in another verdant valley. The place looked almost like a relaxing mountain valley back on Earth. After the Dragon attack and the Orc assault, I wasn't about to let my guard down.

"Another couple of portals and we'll be to our destination." Lead Elf started walking away.

"Wait." I stepped in front of him. "Look, unless Faerie is a lot more dangerous than the tales say it is, something's going on. We didn't come looking for trouble, but it was spilling over into Earth. We had dead Sprites to prove it."

He glared, his face set in a hard mask. I'd run into enough of his type over the years. He wasn't used to people questioning his orders. It made me wonder how high up in the Elven hierarchy he was, or if all Elves were just as snotty.

With a heavy huff, he lowered his eyes first.

Deep inside me, my wolf grinned in triumph.

"You are right, things are spilling over, but this

is not my tale to tell." He glanced at Harris. "If you had not had a powerful mage with you, I'd have just killed you, taken the Djinn by force, and departed your world. We don't normally deal with wolves."

"A little below your notice, most of the time?" I gave him a harsh look and a raised eyebrow.

"Most humans are. You are a strong warrior, and maybe an honorable one."

Rear Elf shouted something I couldn't understand, but he was upset.

Lead Elf held up his hand in a universal sign of 'shut up now'. "I cannot give you all the answers you seek, but I will tell you this. We travel an ever-changing path of portals where we shouldn't be able to be tracked. The Dragons and Orcs are finding us too quickly. We should've been safe. My king and queen will be disturbed by this development, so we must reach them quickly."

Harris put a hand on my arm before I could ask for a better explaination. "Thank you. I know you didn't have to tell us this much. We haven't been properly introduced. I'm Gav-"

"No, mage." Lead Elf put his hand over Harris' mouth and shook his head. "Names have power. Do not give me, or any who may be lurking in earshot that control over you or the wolf." He cast Rear Elf a bit of side-eye, then turned. "With luck, we might find allies as we travel to the next portal. Come, we can't waste time."

I hated the Elves more and more. As much as I was used to just referring to the people around me by last name, or rank, this seemed a bit extreme. Although I recalled Vash saying something about naming things, or maybe it had been Urson. So much magical knowledge and so much of it was new and strange to me.

Lead Elf once again started across the lush green grass. Here and there, trees with purple leaves dotted the landscape along with numerous boulders of white chalky rock. If it hadn't been for the level of threat resting over us, it might've been a nice place to wander for a while and see everything it had to offer, but I wasn't in the mood to run into any more Dragons, Orcs, or even killer rabbits, which seemed more likely in the thick, thigh-high grass.

We'd been walking for nearly an hour when Lead Elf called us to a stop next to a bubbling creek. The water was so clear, it looked like it was going to be super cold.

"We'll rest here for a moment. The water is safe to drink." He pointed toward some boulders resting just shy of the water.

Harris hurried over to the water's edge and dropped to his knees.

I stood back slightly, glancing around. It was one of the better spots for an ambush that we'd come across since we left the slide portal. There was a soft breeze, but nothing seemed ready to jump out at us. That was the perfect time or place to get assaulted.

"He's right." Harris straightened and wiped his hand across his face, knocking a few drops of water off his red beard. "Water's great."

In my time in the Rangers, I'd learned that somebody always kept watch. It was going to be a while before I trusted the Elves enough to do something like bending over to drink without Harris watching out for me.

When Harris had taken another drink, then stood, I finally went over and took a drink. He was right, it was some of the best water I'd ever had, reminding me a lot of the water back at the ranch in Montana.

As I straightened, a warmth spread out from my pockets, and seconds later, Vash's smoke, a bit bluer than normal poured out and she solidified.

Vash glanced around and frowned. "We're in Faerie." She looked up at me. "Lucas, is this what caused you distress a while ago?"

Before I could answer, the sound of swords being yanked out of scabbards jerked my attention away from Vash and to the Elves who didn't look nearly as friendly as they had moments earlier.

"Hey, Dude, it's okay. She'd the Djinn I rescued." I held up my hands and stepped between her and them. "She's on our side." There was definitely more going on than they were telling me. They had known I had a Djinn in my pocket. Why had they drawn swords?

Lead Elf glowered. "How did you come into possession of her vessel? She must-" He cut off and looked around.

"Some being of light told me to protect her." My hand shook slightly with Stormbringer's weight. I couldn't remember drawing the pistol, but it was there pointing towards the Elves. It would just take a slight squeeze and the Elf's head would explode with a bullet for threatening Vash.

Rear Elf sheathed his sword and put a hand on Lead Elf's hand, forcing him to lower his blade as he rattled off something.

Vash frowned and shouted something back at them in their language.

"Hey, can you make it so Har-" I stopped myself from saying Harris's name as I remembered the earlier discussion about the power of names. "We can understand them?"

"Yes." Vash nodded. She made a series of gestures and muttered a couple of soft, sing-song words.

"That's the only explanation," Lead Elf was going on. "But is it safe to take her to the King and Queen?"

"If we do not, it will be our heads on pikes outside the castle wall." Rear Elf pointed at Vash. "They will want to know the earlier attempts failed and she still lives."

We'd missed something very important, but I wasn't sure it would be a good idea to let them know we could understand them thanks to Vash's spell. Had they even noticed her casting it? They were more upset than anything we'd seen before.

From the way Harris was frowning, he was also wondering how Vash was important to the Elves. She was a Djinn, not some kind of Fae, at least not in the way I understood Fae.

Finally, Lead Elf sheathed his sword. "Fine, but if there's trouble it's on your head." He looked at us and switched to English. "Sorry for my actions. I was a little startled by the girl's sudden…
appearance." He looked at Vash and spoke in Elvish, which her spell perfectly translated. "I hope I didn't serve you any offense."

Vash looked a little confused by his words. "My appearance was sudden. I accept your apology."

"Let us continue." He glanced at me. "If we've all had enough to drink."

"I'm good." I glanced at Harris, who just nodded. "We're good to go."

"The next portal isn't very far away." Lead Elf sighed as he jumped gracefully over the creek and continued the way we'd been going.

"Tell me what's happened," Vash's voice was soft, but I bet the Elves could still hear her. Those large pointed ears had to good for something.

Keeping my voice low and steady, I relayed the story after she'd overextended herself and retreated to her bell.

She frowned, then patted my hand. "I'm sorry I wasn't able to help."

"You might be made of magic, but that doesn't mean you have an unlimited supply of energy." I held her hand and squeezed it. "We all have limits."

"Thank you for understanding." She still sounded sad. "Not all of my bearers have been as worldly as you are, Lucas."

Lead Elf glanced over his shoulder, his angular face unreadable as he looked back forward when he realized I'd seen the expression.

Another hour and we'd reached the spot where Lead Elf was going to activate a portal. I wasn't sure what told him where to open the gateways, but none of the ones we'd gone through had been just cast in the air but anchored onto something solid.

"The portal is different than the ones on Earth," Vash touched the towering tree with red needles and yellow bark. If it hadn't been for the strange coloring it could've been a towering redwood. "The energies are more subtle."

Lead Elf cast her a glance. "So you've never been through a portal this deep in Faerie?"

"No." Vash shook her head. "I'm not from Faerie, there's more magic here than I'm used to drawing on."

"There's a lot here you could get used to." Lead Elf passed his hands over the sigils in the bark. They glowed with blue fire as he traced them. "But don't, we'll be returning you and your wolf to Earth as soon as we can."

Although I didn't want to think about how badly I wanted to go home. In all my deployments, I'd never wanted to go home as badly as I did in Faerie. I didn't belong in the strange landscape with weird vegetation, and monsters at every turn. I was a little surprised nothing had jumped out at us while we'd been walking through the peaceful valley. The only life I'd seen had been small butterflies or at least creatures that acted and looked like butterflies. None of them had come close enough for me to get a good look at them, to make sure they weren't smaller Sprites than the ones we'd fought on Earth.

The portal flared open. More silver steaked through the blues that swirled around lights that beckoned us in.

"This is the last portal," Lead Elf took a step back from the event horizon. "We will still have a bit of walking. No portals are allowed to open into the Heart of Faerie. But our journey is nearly at its end."

"Good." I wanted to say something crass about wanting to get off my feet for a while but kept my mouth shut.

"Come on, Lucas." Vash reached for my hand. "It's safe. There's a beautiful land beyond." She sounded more excited than I'd heard her since she re-emerged from her bell.

"Okay. Let's go." I took her hand and for the first time, I entered the portal before Lead Elf. In some ways, it was empowering, although I wasn't totally sure about having him behind me. Vash was back, and that would help balance the scales if things got nasty. I let her lead me through, and we stepped from the green mountain valley through the swirling blue and out onto a stone path winding away and down toward a central court with other paths converging there. A group of Elves with large swords stood in the dead center of the court and they all turned toward us as we cleared the portal. Something in their look said we might not be as welcome as Lead Elf had suggested we would.

As the portal flared again, the Elves drew their swords and started forward.

12

Lead Elf dashed around us and held up his hands to the advancing guards. "Stop, they're with me."

"Captain Yang'fard." The closest guard came to a stop and held up a fist to stop the others. "Why have you brought an abomination and a wolf here? We're at war."

I stiffened. None of them knew I could understand them. That was going to be an advantage, as long as I could keep up the façade. Why did he call Vash an abomination? Did they have some kind of Djinnphobia I didn't understand? Yang'fard had demanded I hand over Vash when we first met but had turned aggressive when she'd appeared. Did the new guy declaring her an abomination have something to do with that? I wanted answers and hoped we'd find them when we reached the king and queen.

Captain Yang'fard, Lead Elf, huffed. "I have my reasons. I must reach the tree. I trust the way is clear."

The new Elf who seemed to be in charge of the guards nodded. "We've pushed back an attempted incursion a couple of hours ago, but it should be clear for you to reach the castle."

"Good." Yang'fard nodded. "Keep your troops here, be ready. We had trouble on the way here, but it's a couple of portals back now. That doesn't mean it won't try to follow us more covertly."

"Understood." The leader of the guard gestured for his unit to let us pass. With a practiced ease I hadn't seen since I had been forced out of the Army, due to being a werewolf, the unit moved to the side as one instead of ten. The simple maneuver made me miss the military more than I had in a few weeks.

Yang'fard strolled past the guards more relaxed than he'd been in the entire trip through the realms. It was going to be a while before I could relax. If all the Elves thought Vash was an abomination, she was in danger, and I had to get her out of there before things got nasty.

We went across the central point where the walks from the portals converged and started down a trail that didn't end in a soft glow. The path was more worn, the rocks smoother than the others, showing it had endured more foot traffic over the centuries. It reached an apex, then swung down. At the top, I stopped and stared at the incredible sight before me.

A giant silver tree rose from the stony ground. The bark of the trunk glistened in the sunlight that seemed to come from everywhere, and nowhere at the same time. For most of the time we'd been walking through the various realms I'd been wondering where the light came from. Never once had I seen a sun or any other obvious source of light, but light there was, and it eluded me. Maybe, if I stopped and thought about it, I'd ask Harris or Vash and see if they knew. I didn't expect the two Elves to answer me correctly, or without scorn for the wolf being stupid.

Huge branches stretched up toward to sunless sky with massive crystals that seemed to grow out of the tree. There was a little bit of difference in each crystal, no two were identical. They ranged from nearly clear to dark smoke with an equal number of reds, blues, purples, and greens.

Harris shook his head. "The Tree of Life. I've heard the stories, but they don't do it justice." A level of reverence vibrated in his tone that I'd never heard him use. "Garnet will be sorry she didn't get to see this. I can just imagine how it would show up in her artwork."

Vash took his hand and smiled up. "I'll be sure to show her. It'll be better than any picture you could take with your phone."

Yang'fard frowned back over his shoulder. "Stop dallying. We have to get you to the court, so they might decide what to do with you."

I sighed. "You guys do realize we were trying to make sure that little Sprite body made it back to where it belonged."

"There's much more going on than you understand, wolf." Yang'fard kept walking down the slope toward the silver tree.

Of that, I didn't doubt. I glanced between Vash and Harris. "Come on, let's see if they'll actually let us know what's going on, or if they'll just keep talking down to us." Other than Urson, the bear alpha in Denver, it seemed like most of the supernaturals involved in the paranormal community loved talking down to anyone who wasn't their kind. Harris didn't do it much, but there were times he had a human-mage view that seemed to place him above things like shifters, or vampires. No matter where we went, tribalism was a real thing. I doubted I would ever be lucky enough to find a place where everyone was on equal footing.

Vash laughed. "Lucas, you're silly."

The way Yang'fard's shoulders stiffened, he didn't appreciate our conversation.

I didn't honestly care, maybe if he or Rear Elf had been a little friendlier, I might've had a different opinion of them. Squeezing Vash's hand, I didn't reply as we continued toward the Tree of Life.

As we drew closer, more details came clear. People, mostly Elves I presumed, moved about the branches, making me realize the crystals were larger than I had expected at my first sight of the tree. There were disks that floated from the ground toward the branches, or between branches. They looked like some kind of magic helped move them around. Here and there, people stared down from the branches, watching us approach. It sent shivers through me. My military training screamed that we were exposed and easy targets if anyone on a branch had a gun, bow, or even a rock.

"They're all looking at us," Vash whispered like she was afraid someone would hear her.

"We're probably very different from what they're used to seeing around here." I kept hold of her hand, ready to defend her if something happened.

A wooden staircase spiraled up the outside of the tree. It was nearly the same silver color of bark covering the tree. The treads were an easy pacing. Yang'fard started up and didn't pause to see if any of the rest of us were following. I wished he would slow down and give us a chance to look around, but I understood that the less we saw, the less chance we could find weaknesses in their defenses.

Working our way up the tree, as we passed various branches, more and more people were standing there looking at us. Up close, they were more than just Elves. If I had to guess there were a few Dwarves among them, along with some kind of willowy Fae that looked like a cross between a water beetle and a gibbon, with a humanoid face and six hairy limbs. Sprites and other winged Fae flitted around the tree trunk, curious, but staying out of sword range.

When we were about a quarter of the way up, my legs were already starting to complain about the strain of climbing. Harris was huffing a bit, sounding even more strained.

Yang'fard stepped off the stairs at a large landing that extended into the tree's body. Across the landing, a door that stood nearly ten feet tall with delicate carvings of two Elves waited for us. There were four guards, two on each side standing there, looking more dangerous than any Elves I'd encountered to that point, even the unit at the portal round-about we'd come through. They were taller than Yang'fard, or Rear Elf, and broader, looking a lot like the Orc, at least in the shoulder. They held long halberd swords with hafts and blades that looked like they could do a lot of damage before the guards ever got into hand-to-hand range with most opponents. If I was right, there were daggers in their belts, sleeves, and boots. Across the back of the closest two, were bows and quivers full of arrows. If they were any kind of fighter at all, I didn't want to have to try to take on one of them, let alone four.

The closest one on the right stepped in front of us. "Captain Yang'fard, a message has reached the king. He is waiting for you." He held out a couple of leather straps.

Taking the straps, Yang'fard nodded. "Of course." He looked at me. "Wolf, hold out your arm."

I stared at him. "Why?"

"You carry magical weapons. You yourself are a magical weapon. It is imperative that you speak with the king about the Djinn you control. I cannot allow you in his presence without being sure you do not present him with a danger."

"My word isn't good enough for you?" I didn't like the idea of being neutered to speak with the Elf king. If I had to, I would. I was an ex-Army Ranger. Even without the wolf curled deep in my mind, I was a weapon all on my own. I could give a hardcore attempt to protect Vash.

A clouded look crossed Yang'fard's features. "I haven't had time to measure your honor. Please make this easier on all of us." He glanced at Vash. "We will also be blocking the Djinn and the mage."

"Are we prisoners?" It would be stupid to just let him put the band on me, somehow, I bet it was a lot tougher than it appeared.

"That's not for me to decide." Yang'fard he dropped his voice. "Please, Lucas, don't make this difficult. If you don't agree, I will take the Djinn and allow the king to decide her fate without any input from you or the mage."

Chills went through me. He was dead serious. The Elf would kill me. Vash was the only thing important to him, and I was fairly sure in much different ways than she was to me. I remembered Agent Briar, the werewolf who ran a black ops unit for the FBI, had threatened to kill me, take her bell, and lock a potentially dangerous weapon away. I wasn't going to let that happen if I could. "Okay." I held out my arm.

"You are new enough as a wolf, that you can see reason." Yang'fard encircled my wrist with the leather band.

It didn't look too bad.

Magic surged through me. Every silver hair on my body stood straight out. Deep inside, my wolf's howl of outrage was cut off. I couldn't feel him. For the first time in months, I was alone in my soul. If I'd been a weaker man, I'd have screamed. The loneliness was nearly painful. I wanted to hit Yang'fard. Punch him so hard that I'd break those pretty Elven cheekbones, but I resisted. I had to. For Vash.

I shook my head and glared at Yang'fard. "You realize if you hurt her, I will do worse to you."

"You will try." Yang'fard knelt in front of Vash. "Now you, little Djinn. It will block your magic, but still allow you a physical form."

With her hands on her hips and a dark pout on

her lips, she looked between us. "But you hurt, Lucas."

"Wolves are more delicate than Djinn." Yang'fard held out his hand for hers. "You'll be okay."

Harris sighed. "Put mine on first. Show her I won't be hurt. I doubt you'd survive if she blasted you off this part of the tree."

Shaking his head, Yang'fard rose. "I doubt you would either."

I understood the posturing. It was one of the few things that carried over from Ranger to werewolf, and apparently to Elves, but it wasn't getting us anywhere. "Vash, it'll be okay. I can still hurt him if he or any of the other Elves try anything stupid."

She smiled slightly. "I know you would."

After Harris got his band with no obvious pain, she held out her hand and accepted hers. "I know how to hurt you too." As the sparks from her hair faded away, she flashed Yang'fard the most diabolical smile I'd ever seen her use. It made me wonder where she had learned that. The look wasn't one I'd seen on Garnet or Cin, maybe one of her previous carriers had a wife who used those kinds of looks.

Then we were ready. The guard Elf stepped back and let Yang'fard lead us through the doors and into what could only be described as the most organic throne room ever built.

13

At the far end of the room, a pair of chairs, not as big as I had expected thrones to be, grew out of the floor. The silver sheen of both pieces of furniture was reminiscent of the great tree's bark. In foot-long squares, the floor tiles to either side of a central walk were softly different from each other. The central walk looked like someone had managed to catch a stream in mid-babble, freeze it in time, and lay it on the floor. Even as we walked down it, I wasn't sure what it was made of since my hiking boots didn't make the least little sound as I put my feet down. Various tapestries kept drawing my momentary attention with their bright colors depicting scenes of valor, mostly Elves fighting things like Dragons and other huge beasts I couldn't identify.

Then the woman on the left chair moved, drawing attention to her. Before she'd moved, she'd blended in more than the man next to her, but when she shifted slightly and looked down toward us, she separated herself from the carved elegance around her and stood out like a swan among geese. She took even my breath away. Her long silver hair was a perfect complement to the throne she rested in. Her cheekbones were sharper than Yang'fard's, but not in an underfed, drawn way; they served to accent her face, making it look delicate to the point of fragile. Her ice-blue eyes settled on Vash. Something flashed there, almost a look of recognition. She put her hands on the arms of her chair and started to stand until the man seated to her right put his own hand on hers.

"Wait." The word was just above a whisper, but the room's acoustics were so perfect, it carried to me, even without me being able to access my wolf side.

Yang'fard stopped us a few feet from the dais the chairs rose from. "Your majesties. I bring the Djinn, wolf, and mage as you requested."

I kept my face frozen. During our journey through the realms, I hadn't been aware of any communication between Yang'fard and anyone, but there must have been some kind of Elf magic that I didn't know about that allowed them to pass orders back and forth. Maybe that was why we were standing in their throne room and not left at the bottom of the cliffs the Dragons had come from. If someone would have just provided me with the intel on everything that kept intruding on my life, I'd have been happy to study it so I didn't feel like I was constantly playing catch-up with the magical world.

"Thank you, Yang'fard." The man moved slightly in the chair. He was nearly as pretty as the queen, but there were little touches, like his hint of a beard, that was more of a dark gray pencil-thin goatee. He didn't have the softness she displayed, right down to a scar on his left cheek. I wondered if it was from a real battle, like the ones displayed on the tapestries, or if it was something more trivial. I had gotten too used to rulers who couldn't be bothered with fighting their own battles, people who let their soldiers risk their lives while they sat safe and sound continents away.

Harris took a step forward. "Your majesties, this is a great honor."

The king held up a hand. "We will get to you, mage." His blue eyes darkened as he looked at me. "Wolf, what is your name?"

Names. Harris and Yang'fard had both cautioned about names, but I had no doubt that if I lied, he would somehow know it. I didn't move forward, but inclined my head slightly, hoping it was enough to appease him. I wanted us all to get out of the room in one piece. "David Lucas, your majesty."

The king eased back in his chair. "David Lucas, well met. If Yang'fard hasn't already informed you, and I doubt he has, I am An'Fa'el, king of the Lum'se'el, what your people call Light Elves." He held out his hand to the woman sitting next to him. "This is my wife and queen, Yas'Fe'el"

Copying Harris' wording, I again inclined my head to the queen. "We are honored, your majesties."

"Mr. Lucas," An'Fa'el began, holding onto the queen's hand like he was trying to remind her he was there and needed to be in control of the situation. "You are the bearer of the Djinn's vessel?"

Although he didn't appear to have looked at Vash, Yas'Fe'el hadn't taken her gaze off her.

"I am." As I let the words out, I half expected either one of them or some hidden guard or mage to strike me down and take Vash's bell from my corpse.

"Tell me how you came to be in possession of it." His gaze swept over me and seemed to linger on my leg where the bell rested in my pocket.

Not exactly sure how much I should reveal, I glanced at Harris.

He nodded. "These are the good guys."

If the situation had been different, I might've laughed. Good guys killed people too, they just always did it for 'good and just' reasons. Everyone was the hero of their own tale. "I was fighting some Effrits, dark Djinn, in Afghanistan on Earth. A being of light, I still don't know what he was, said she liked me and I should protect her."

An'Fa'el glanced at Yas'Fe'el, a look of surprise on his face. "Protect. He used that term. You are sure."

Vash stepped just in front of me and glared up at the Elves. "Of course he did. Lucas is my protector. I am *not* his slave. He is the best bearer I have ever had. He's like a father to me." The leather band on her wrist burned away and angry red sparks cascaded down her hair.

Beside us, Yang'fard and Rear Elf gasped softly and reached for their swords.

Ignoring them, the queen straightened. "And your story, child?" Yas'Fe'el shook off An'Fa'el's hand. "Who were your real parents? How did you become trapped in your vessel?"

Vash looked at me and stepped back. "I've been a Djinn my whole life. I don't remember not being bound. But sometimes, when I'm lost in the quiet emptiness of my bell, I remember a strong heady smoke, like frankincense. There is normally a hint of green, like growing plants and the earth."

Yas'Fe'el slipped off her throne and knelt just off the dais, holding her arms out to Vash. "Come to me, child, let me feel you."

Conflicting emotions went through me. I was totally lost about what was happening. The queen seemed to know something she wasn't totally revealing to the rest of us. Or maybe all the Elves knew something they weren't going to let the wolf and mage in on.

Again, Vash looked up at me.

Not seeing a safe way to do anything else, I nodded and prepared to throw myself at the Elf woman if something strange happened.

Nervous pale sparks flowed off Vash as she took a couple of steps forward.

The queen wrapped her arms around Vash, like a relative might, giving her a brief hug.

Slowly, Vash returned the embrace.

Still on his throne, the king stiffened.

Like he was picking up on something I couldn't, Yang'fard looked around.

A chill ran through me. I wanted the leather bracelet off. Something was happening.

Harris's blond eyebrows rose and he gripped his staff. "What's that?"

"What, Harris? What's happening?" I pulled at the leather, but it was stronger than it looked.

Three portals opened around the room. The magic came as a wash of power.

"This isn't possible." Yang'fard's Elvish words

were shouted as he yanked his sword free of its scabbard.

"We are breached." An'Fa'el stood and shouted. "To arms!"

Elves came through the portals, at least a dozen. They were more rugged and dangerous looking than the Elves in the tree had been. There was no doubt they were hardened warriors.

Rear Elf was closest to them. He shouted something that didn't translate as he rushed forward, his sword held out like a lance.

Yas'Fe'el moved to stand in front of Vash.

I tried to pull Stormbringer from his holster, but the gun didn't come out. It was stuck. Then I understood that the magic of the bracelet kept me from drawing weapons in the presence of the royalty. It didn't simply neutralize my wolf, it blocked all my offensive capabilities.

Holding out my arm, I looked at Vash as Yas'Fe'el began some kind of magical gesturing and the attacking Elves rushed toward them. "Vash, take this thing off me."

She smiled as she pointed at me. Her own magic was more subtle and packed a bigger punch than the Elf power. The leather on my wrist flamed, burning some of the silver hairs there, then dropped away.

Deep inside me, my wolf surged up, snarling.

My senses flared, I could tell where all the attackers were, where the defenders were, and the easy difference between them. There were small differences between them, things my wolf could make out and relay to me.

I jerked Stormbringer out as Yang'fard engaged

an Elf, easily parrying his blow before running him through like something out of a sword and sorcery movie. Spinning toward the next closest one, I targeted.

Stormbringer thundered through the throne room, then the bullet struck the Elf I'd been aiming at and his head exploded.

The doors of the throne room flew open. Two guards rushed in, but the sounds of battle came from the entry room. There were attackers all over the tree, or at least on that level.

A new portal opened near the throne.

Yas'Fe'el threw up a shield that deflected a fireball that came toward her and Vash.

With a gesture, Vash returned the fireball toward the attacker.

Elves and Effrit came through the new portal. They didn't bother heading toward anyone but Vash and Yas'Fe'el.

I rushed toward them, switching my magazine out for magical rounds. Regular bullets might give the Effrit a little discomfort, but I wasn't looking for a little discomfort. If there were Effrit coming through, they were after Vash. I had to take them down before they could get to her.

The magazine clicked into place as an Elf with a huge sword tried to cut me off.

Without a thought, or slowing in my step, I brought Stormbringer up and fired. Lightning danced out from the barrel and exploded the Elf more spectacularly than anything I'd ever seen.

"You must get her to safety." Yas'Fe'el took Vash's hand and pushed her toward me. "She is precious to us."

Vash didn't need any urging, she took my hand.

"But where's safe?" I took out the closest Effrit as it swooped down toward us like a smoky, skeletal vulture.

"Yang'fard, get them out of here!" Yas'Fe'el cast a shield, then made a complicated series of gestures, casting a portal with nothing anchoring it.

"Yes, my queen." Yang'fard bowed.

The guards from the door formed up around the dais, some of them fighting with their long halberds, some using magic. An'Fa'el stood, his long blue sleeves billowing as he cast spell after spell. Some of them hit what he was aiming at, and a few went wide, exploding on the wall behind an Elf or Effrit. They were making a royal mess of the audience chamber.

Yang'fard glanced at me and Harris. "Come."

He dashed toward the portal Yas'Fe'el had crafted.

Not needing to be told twice, I held onto Vash's hand as I popped off a couple more bullets at oncoming Elves and dark Djinn. There was a growing list of things I wanted answers to, but first, we needed to get somewhere safe. I hoped he was taking us back to Earth. I wanted a chance to get my feet under me and understand what was going on.

A fireball shattered Yas'Fe'el's shield. The Elf queen dropped to her knees.

Pausing at the portal's event horizon, I got off another shot, as Vash let a fireball fly. The Elf that had gotten through the queen's defenses was blasted to ash as our joint attack hit home.

Yang'fard grabbed my arm. "Come on, Lucas. If Vash dies, the queen will have my head." He jerked us into the portal and the battle died around us.

Before I could get my bearings, Harris stepped into the room we found ourselves in. He looked a bit frazzled. His shoulder-length hair stood out, frazzeled, and there were scorch marks on his bright T-shirt.

I jerked my arm out of Yang'fard's grasp. "Do you mind telling us what's going on?"

14

As the portal closed, Yang'fard glanced around. It was a familiar action. He was making sure we were safe. When he frowned, a stab of fear surged through me. "We need to keep moving."

I caught his arm. "Look, I've been going along with this whole thing, because I wanted to help a Sprite and Harris seemed to be okay with this, but Vash is in danger. I need answers."

"Yes." Yang'fard nodded. "And I'll give you what I know when we are safe. This place isn't far from the royal chambers. We need to keep moving." He gently pulled out of my grasp and touched the wall that was etched with familiar marks. "This shouldn't be here. Let's see where it goes." As he'd done before, he triggered the runes slowly.

"You don't know where the portal goes?" I didn't like the sound of that. Following him before had been easy because he'd always felt like he'd known where our next step would land. I wasn't in the mood for more uncertainty.

"I've never used this one before, and it's set for a particular location. I can't alter that." He glanced over his shoulder and met my gaze. "You're going to have to keep trusting me, Lucas. My lieges want

Vash safe. I won't let anything happen to you, or her." He finished activating the portal. It glowed with a soft red fire. The color was unlike any of the portals we'd stepped through before.

"Lucas, he's got a point." Harris patted my shoulder. "And I hate to say it, but at this point, I'm so lost I doubt either Vash, or I could get us home without a native guide."

That's part of what I'd been afraid of. "I know."

"Come on." Yang'fard motioned us forward, then stepped through the portal.

We didn't have Rear Elf anymore. There was nothing or no-one to force us to follow him. But there didn't appear to be any other way out of the room. It didn't even have a door or any furniture. It was probably the Elven equivalent to a safe room or bolt-hole. With my heavy sigh, hoping we would end up somewhere we wouldn't have anyone attacking us, I took hold of Vash's hand again and stepped through.

We found ourselves in a room that looked like some kind of small cabin, complete with two narrow beds, and the Elven equivalents of kitchen conveniences. The sink and stove had a window over them. The table and chairs looked to be made from the same silvery wood as the thrones and dais we'd left behind.

Yang'fard was already walking toward a cabinet like he hadn't been worried we wouldn't follow him. With nowhere else to go, he probably had little to worry about.

"We should be safe here, at least for a little while, depending on how focused they are on reaching, Vash." He opened the cabinet, revealing a cold box that was filled with bottles and food. "I think we should have some nourishment. We've been on the trail for a long time."

"Sounds good." I nodded as my stomach rumbled reminding me that I couldn't subsist on adrenalin alone.

Yang'fard pulled out several bottles of something and carried them to the table, then returned to the fridge and removed plates of meat.

The bottles were twist tops, and I opened one and passed it to Vash, before opening my own. The liquid inside tasted like weak lemonade. As it traveled down my throat, it spread an invigorating cool through my system.

Harris grabbed a couple of pieces of meat, and just ate them like jerky, with his fingers. "Okay, Yang'fard, what's going on? This seems like more than just a bit of conflict between the Elf factions."

I took some of the meat, not instantly recognizing what it was from, but figuring it didn't matter, as long as it wasn't somehow poisonous to us. "This feels a bit more like a full-scale war."

"It is." Yang'fard set a loaf of cold bread next to the meats and proceeded to make himself a sandwich. "As far back as any of us can remember the Dark Elf clans, we call them Hun'se, have been at war with the Lum'se'el."

"Wait no 'el on the end. Is that significant?" It might be nothing, but as I was trying to understand what was going on, it might help me understand things when I stumbled over them.

A soft smile formed on the Elf's face. "The 'el

suffix means Elf. Although there is a common link, many thousands of years ago, we no longer consider them an Elf clan, so we no longer use the 'el when referring to them."

"But you do not have the 'el like the king and queen do." The meat was very tasty, and if I'd been in a human home, I would have been polite and made a sandwich too, but I didn't want to risk diluting the taste with bread.

"They embody the entire Light Elf culture. The rest of us don't have the honor of the extra suffix." Yang'fard took a drink.

"That's useful to know." Harris smiled as he finished off his meat and reached for some bread. "So the clans split thousands of years ago and have been at war ever since. Are things getting worse?"

Yang'fard nodded. "Correct, mage. We don't understand everything that's happening in their court, but they've suddenly allied themselves with any who are willing to stand against us. We fear that they might be planning something huge. After we felt some of their energies on Earth, I sent a squad of Sprites to investigate. One of their operatives caught them and destroyed almost all of them before they could report back."

"Which is where the Sprite we found came from." I reached for more meat. The bread held little interest for my wolf who pressed against my skin, as eager for food and information as I was.

"Right," Harris said before Yang'fard could. "But why didn't it go back to Faerie when it died? That's the part that I don't understand."

"Nor do I." Yang'fard took another sip from his

bottle.

"Djinn magic," Vash offered. "Maybe the Hun'se had an Effrit with him. We can stop things from moving from one realm to another."

"And that is one of the more disturbing things that's going on." Yang'fard frowned as he set his bottle down on the table, then paced slightly as he held his sandwich. "According to our sources, the Effrit were the first group the Hun'se allied themselves with. Djinn magic must've been what allowed them to pierce the barrier around the Tree of Life. Without their help, they never would've reached so deep into our realm."

"We've fought Effrit on Earth," I said.

"They were after me." Vash looked at me. "Is that why they attacked the tree, to get me?"

I shrugged. "We might never know." I glanced at Yang'fard. "Any idea what's so important? When you first saw her, you started at her."

Yang'fard pursed his lips. "I was hoping my lieges would explain, but I suppose it falls on me."

At last, we were going to get some answers. Maybe with all the data, I could construct a way to protect Vash from the craziness that had become our life.

The wall where the portal was shimmered before Yang'fard could say more.

I pulled Stormbringer out and aimed it at the spot. Beside me, Yang'fard had dropped his sandwich on the floor and had his sword free.

Rear Elf stumbled through the portal, covered in blood, a chipped sword in his grip.

"Slyl'fard, what happened?" Yang'fard caught

the other Elf in his arms, then helped him over to a chair.

"The Hun'se and their allies were almost too much to repel." He pushed out the words between ragged gasps.

Harris handed him an open bottle of the weak lemonade from the fridge. "Drink this."

"Thanks, mage." Slyl'fard took the bottle and took a sip.

Yang'fard knelt before his friend. "Our forces held?"

"After losses, yes." Slyl'fard nodded. "It's been many centuries since I've seen a battle so bloody. Yang, it was awful." His voice cracked and he took another sip of the bottle.

As I holstered Stormbringer, his words rang in my head. He'd said centuries. I glanced down at Vash who was standing silently at my side. She was more than two thousand years old, even though she looked like she was only eight. Since Djinn aged differently than humans, it made sense that some other other-worldly species might as well. The tales of the Fae spoke of them living for a long time, but it was still a lot to process, and the idea that these two warriors had existed so long, made me feel like a child. The things they must know and understand that I was just seeing the hints of.

"Yli'lian was slain." Slyl'fard shook and tears streaked through the blood on his face as he spoke.

Yang'fard gapped. "The princess. How is that possible?"

Slyl'fard bowed and shook his head. "I don't know how she knew to come, but I can guess why."

He cast a fast glance toward Vash. "She made it to the throne room seconds after you left. The dark ones over whelmed her. The queen valiantly tried to reach her."

Growling, Yang'fard hit the wooden floor hard. "But the king and queen survive?"

"Thank the tree, yes." Slyl'fard looked up into Yang'fard's face. "The queen. I've heard tales of the beauty she can be when she fights, but I never truly understood. Now I do. If I die this day, I at least got to see her at her finest, most deadly. Her spells were only outdone by her swordplay. The king is but a shadow to her light. When the princess fell, she became like a swooping hawk, deadly and lovely at the same time. Never shall there be another like her."

If it hadn't been for protecting Vash, it sounded like a sight to behold. In some ways, I was sorry that I'd missed it.

Slyl'fard finished off his bottle. "We should return. The threat is passed for the moment. We are going to press an attack soon, and the king and queen want all of us back."

"No." I shook my head. "You need to get Vash, Harris, and me back home. Once you do that, and we're safe, you can come back and wage your war. We're not part of it."

Yang'fard stood and squared his shoulders. "David Lucas, you are part of this, even if you don't understand that yet."

"Then maybe you can make us understand." I hated people telling me I didn't understand something when I already knew that I didn't have all the intel.

The two Elves looked at each other. "We should tell them." Slyl'fard reverted to Elvish.

Deep inside, a warm note of happiness that they didn't realize we could understand them.

"It's not our tale to tell." Yang'fard took a step back and glared at Slyl'fard.

"The princess is dead," Slyl'fard glared at him, the tears slowly drying in the streaked blood. "The king or queen could tell, but they are rallying our troops. They don't have time."

"And we don't have the right." Yang'fard curled his hands into tight fists.

"The right to tell us what?" Vash took a couple of steps away from my side, and the sparks tumbling from her hair grew bright red. "I could get the information from you if I needed to."

Hiding the grin that wanted to spread across my face, I put a hand on her shoulder. "I think she understands you." I wanted to hide my own knowledge of their tongue as long as I could.

Yang'fard spun and stared at her. "It is easy to forget you're here."

Vash cocked her head. "Djinn are mostly smoke and air. We are easy to forget or ignore. Many have learned over the years that we are forgotten at great peril."

I couldn't help but smile. It was impossible to say who her words were coming from, me, or any of the strong women around her, but Vash was becoming very much a child of our time, and not a subservient girl ready to let the men around her talk and not speak her mind. I hoped she could feel how proud of her I was at that moment.

"Your mother was our princess," Slyl'fard blurted out. "She was on her way to the throne room when the attack happened."

That was something I hadn't been expecting. Was it possible for an Elf to become a Djinn? How did that even work? At every turn, there was more and more about the supernatural world I didn't understand, but that had to be one of the biggest surprises, even if it did explain why the queen had reacted the way she did when she'd met Vash. But, was that also the reason the Effrit were so determined to kill Vash?

15

"My mother?" Vash glanced at me, then stared at Yang'fard. "How is that possible?"

Yang'fard started pacing.

"You might want to answer her." I wanted answers too. If Yang'fard didn't want to give them, maybe Slyl'fard would. I stared from one Elf to the other. Deep inside my wolf growled, wanting to come out and force the Elves to tell us what we wanted to know.

"Magic." Harris took a seat at the table. "Your parents must've used magic to create you."

"We may never know exactly what happened." Yang'fard stopped pacing and came over to kneel in front of Vash. "Please believe me that I didn't know who you were when we first met. All I saw was an abomination that shouldn't exist."

My head spun at his choice of words. "Wait…what?"

"Yang, please be quiet and let me explain. You're apt to make things worse." Slyl'fard finished off his drink and set the bottle on the table. "This cautionary story goes back many thousands of years before either one of us was born, but I've heard it many times, even told it to my own children to warn them about mixing their blood with that of other races. You see, like humans, not all of the Fae are created equal."

"Don't go there." I held up a hand. "Humans have enough racial problems without people outside our species adding to them. Stick to the Fae part of this story." We didn't have time for an Elf to start spouting racial bluster.

"Sorry." Slyl'fard looked at me and bowed slightly. "Back to Fae history. Different races, or species if you prefer, have different levels of magic, all with limitations. If we don't have limits then it's too easy for war to break out."

"I can understand that." I nodded and put my hands behind my back, almost defaulting to a parade rest stance to listen to him.

"Even the Dragons, one of the most powerful races, have limits to their power. From time to time, because we do almost everything from the angle of growing power, there are…missteps made. The Djinn are among the powerful races of what you call supernatural, or paranormal creatures. Their ultimate limitation is that things they create with their magic only last a day. Yes, they can create great magical things, but since they only last a short period of time, they cannot, on their own, take over a realm and create a place of power to strike out at others."

"So no castles and things like that." Again, I understood that. Vash had explained it while we'd been looking for a home. Sure, she could make us a house, but it would fade away at dawn the next day. It wasn't practical and made perfectly good sense to me.

"Exactly," Slyl'fard continued. "Elves are great creators. We can make things like castles, libraries, the portal network, and such, but it takes us time. We don't have the raw power the Djinn or Dragons have. Many times, it has been just as easy to build with our hands as with our magic, much like humans do."

I chuckled. I'd seen their Tree of Life. There was no way humans could ever build something so incredible.

"When humans were first learning to stand upright, before they saw us as an enemy, we grew tired of the time it took to build things like the great wall, and other monuments to our greatness. So some of our greatest thinkers of the time approached the Djinn, and we learned how to mingle blood with them." Slyl'fard looked at Vash. "Not all of those minglings ended well. Some of those early attempts were easy enough to destroy before they got out of control. Others…" Slyl'fard bowed and shook his head. "Blood ran through the realms at that time. Many realms were so damaged that to this day, they aren't safe for long exposure. Nothing but nightmares inhabit those places and we leave them be as a warning of what should never be again."

"And yet, your princess did." I put a hand on Vash's shoulder and pulled her against my legs.

"I am not a monster who would destroy entire realms." Vash looked up at me, and then back to Slyl'fard.

The bloody Elf smiled. "From what I have seen, that is true."

"When we first saw you, we weren't so sure."

Yang'fard leaned against the table. "We are sworn to protect Faerie, even things like Orcs, from outside forces that might do us harm. I saw you as such."

Harris pointed his finger thoughtfully. "Wait a moment. That mage, the one who we fought on the burn scar. There was something different about him. Is it possible he could also be a hybrid?"

"For a long time, the Hun'se have sought a source of power that would let them overwhelm the Great Tree." Slyl'fard glanced at Yang'fard. "It is possible they have such a creature at their disposal."

Vash stamped her foot. Definitely, something she learned from Cin or Garnet. "I am not a creature."

I patted her shoulder. "No, you're not."

"I apologize for my wording." Slyl'fard gave Vash a low bow. "Such things are ingrained in many of us. Please have patience."

"Maybe." Vash swooshed her hair and more amber sparks than normal fell from her red tresses.

I chuckled and patted her shoulder again. "That's my girl."

"Please, continue," Harris prompted. "This is very interesting. I'd heard of other Elven crosses, but not Djinn."

"Other than Dragons, it is the most dangerous," Slyl'fard sounded like he was going to start again, but I held up a hand.

"Whoa. There are Dragon hybrids? Do I even want to know how that worked…works?" Yeah, things were getting stranger.

"Although they are rare and keep to themselves, Dragon/Elf hybrids do exist; it is where the occasional Dragon shifters come from. Unlike your wolf, Dragons are not contagious to humans." Yang'fard closed his eyes and shook his head. "If they were, your world and ours would be a much different place."

"Something to keep an eye out for." Harris nodded and had the look of someone who was totally enjoying the info-dump we were enduring and wished he had a pen and paper, or computer, to make notes on.

Having dealt with Dragons already, I wasn't sure I wanted to see what a Dragon shifter could do.

"About two thousand years ago, there were rumors surrounding Princess Yli'lian. She was young, just coming into her full power. Some claimed she'd been seduced by a masterless Djinn, and they were trying to find a way to have a child of power." Slyl'fard again looked at Vash as he folded his hands in his lap. "Although she often had the energy of a Djinn on her, there was never any evidence that they had done anything…obscene…"

Vash stamped her foot again but stayed silent.

Slyl'fard continued, "Even when they were caught together, there was no proof of a child's existence, although both were frantic. The Djinn removed him and the Elves took the princess back to her parents. She stayed with them until all possible threat had passed. During that time, she'd fallen into a melancholy that lasted for a thousand years. Then one day, she again began gardening and slowly returned to normal."

"She smelled of flowers and earth." Vash looked up at me, and tiny tears sparkled in her eyes.

"Her voice was almost like bird song." Her lower lip quivered. "She… she… glowed… with a… a… green energy."

I knelt and took her in my arms. She'd never cried before. Sure I'd only known her a few months, but she'd never cried. Wrapping her arms around my neck, she sobbed. The sparks coming from her hair changed from their regular yellow, orange, and red to dull blue. It was the most like a preteen child that she'd ever been. I hugged her until her tears slowed to a stop and her sparks returned to subdued hue of their normal.

Sniffling, Vash wiped her nose with the back of her hand.

I wished I'd had a handkerchief to loan her.

When she was a little composed, Vash looked at me. "Lucas, we have to help them. She was my mother." Vash closed her eyes like she was fighting another wave of tears. "We have to do something."

If it had been my mother, I'd have felt the same way. I stroked her hair and then wiped a couple of tears from her puffy, flushed cheeks. "Okay, sweetie. We'll make those Dark Elves pay."

Taking her in my arms, I stood and looked at Yang'fard and Slyl'fard. "We'll help. No binding magic. We're going in there with guns blazing and when this is all done, you're getting us back to Earth. Do I make myself clear?"

Yang'fard nodded. "Crystal."

We had a target, or targets as the case was. I always felt on more stable ground when I had a target in my sights.

16

As we started back toward the court, Yang'fard and Slyl'fard stopped in their tracks and got a faraway look that reminded me of how a telepath, who had helped us find Vash when she'd been kidnapped, looked when he'd been communicating with others.

Vash tugged my hand. "The court is calling everyone together. The queen is declaring a war against the Hun'se."

Yang'fard stared at Vash. "You heard her? Her call went out to the Light Fae."

"And I think you just explained to us, that Vash is part Fae." I focused on the Elves but put a hand on Vash's shoulder. "If she's part Fae, Light Fae, why shouldn't she be in this magical network?"

The two Elves looked at each other and reverted to their language.

"This proves she is one of us," Slyl'fard said first.

"That is not for us to decide." Yang'fard frowned hard.

"We're wasting time." I still didn't want them knowing I could understand them, although Vash had already let them know she could. If they continued discounting her, and me, that would help us out in the long term.

Slyl'fard nodded. "You're right. The wide portal network is coming down. We need to move."

The small room wasn't somewhere I wanted to be stuck in. But I wondered if Vash and Harris would be able to get us out of there if that happened. Yang'fard had been opening portals, but if the portals were part of a network, then it might be possible to just lock it down if I understood how the magic worked.

With a series of quick gestures, Yang'fard created a portal on the wall. "Let's go."

I kept hold of Vash's hand as we stepped through the swirling magic

Dead leaves crunched underfoot as we stepped from the portal to the Tree of Life. Moans of pain drew my attention as we hurried toward the throne room. Here and there Elves, Sprites, and other Fae lay waiting for help. I'd seen enough fighting over the years that I could turn my head and keep going.

"Lucas." Vash stopped and pulled on my hand. "We have to help. I can-"

Stopping, I knelt and looked deep into her green eyes that sparkled with Djinn magic. "I know you could help, but right now we need to see the king and queen, your grandparents. They might need your power more than these people here do."

She stuck out her lower lip and shook her head. "I don't like it."

"It was a fierce battle. You're not supposed to like it." I hugged her. "If you did, there would be something wrong with you."

Harris patted us both on the shoulder. "Come on, our escorts are looking concerned about something."

That wasn't surprising. Walking into a city you'd lived in to find it scarred from an attack of enemy forces couldn't be easy. "Let's keep going." I stood and kept hold of Vash's hand. "Let's see where the royals need us. I know we can help with things."

Vash let out a heavy sigh and set her shoulders in a stubborn angle. "Okay, but we have to help these people. It's not their fault the Hun'se are such awful people." She was definitely picking up a lot from the strong women we had around us.

I wasn't sure the magical world was ready for a no-nonsense modern Djinn girl who just might turn into a crusader if I let her. I smiled as we continued walking toward the throne room. At least it was better than a subservient person, the way the Djinn were normally portrayed in modern entertainment. In a few years, the supernatural world might not know what had hit it.

The guards at the throne-room doors leaned heavily on their polearms. The one on the left raised tired eyes toward us. Dried blood ran down his face from a nasty cut just under his hairline. He didn't say anything, just pushed the door open so we could enter. A heavy bandage wrapped his hand, distorting its shape like he was missing fingers or something.

My wolf stirred as the cloying scent of blood hit

me. I pushed back the urge to growl.

Shadows replaced the light that had filled the chamber before. Even the queen, talking to a couple of women near her throne, didn't radiate elegance and perfection as she had previously. Her long flowing hair was tangled and a smudge of blood that didn't look like it was her own spotted her cheek.

One of the women she spoke with, muttered something, then nodded toward us.

Yas'Fe'el turned toward us and watched as we strode across the audience chamber. "Yang'fard, Slyl'fard, thank you for returning our guests to our presence."

"As you command." The two Elves bowed in unison.

Vash looked at me with a question in her eyes, silently asking if we should bow as well.

Beside us, Harris did, but I wasn't in the mood to. Sure, I'd agreed to lend a hand with their problem, but I didn't want to seem like Vash and I were there to be ordered around by the Elf queen and her people.

Yas'Fe'el's gaze on me was a little more hostile than I liked, but it didn't matter. "We are not going to let this assault on our realm or the death of our daughter go unanswered. Mr. Lucas, as much as we'd prefer to keep Vash safe, we feel her power will be needed. So far our pleas to the Light Djinn go unanswered. The Hun'se had Effrits aiding them. We need a way to counter that power."

"It sounds like you're asking my permission." I did my best to not come across like I was trying to challenge her, as much as my wolf wanted to growl at her. "Vash is her own person. If she wants to help you, I'll be there to back her up."

A line of confusion crossed her smooth forehead. "But you are her guardian."

"And as such, I guard her—" I put a hand on her shoulder. "—and I *will* make sure that she's safe. But our involvement in your fight is up to her. I don't have a stake in this."

"Oh, we might," Harris interrupted. "If the Dark Fae and Effrit take over Faerie, it's only a matter of time before their forces reach Earth and start trouble there."

If we hadn't been standing there before the queen, I'd have explained to Harris that I understood that. But we needed a uniform front to keep our stance stronger.

"Lucas." Vash looked at me again, with the pleading sparkle in her eyes. "We have to help."

Yas'Fe'el swept her silver gown out, then squatted in front of us, holding her hands out to Vash. "You have the bearing and command of a future queen. I would appreciate the power you wield to be used for our side."

"Then we shall." Vash looked from the queen to me. "Won't we, Lucas?"

I nodded. "We shall." I wasn't sure what it was going to involve and wished we had time to go back to Earth and get loaded up on every magical bullet Urson could craft for Stormbringer. I worried I might run out of ammo before we made it back to a portal to Earth.

17

The small room on a nearby limb, that we'd been taken to, reminded me a little of the room we'd ended up in. There wasn't a kitchenette, or whatever the Elves called it, but there were a few chairs and a long table. It reminded me of a boardroom, if a boardroom had an overly organic feel. The table looked like it had grown out of the floor. Two benches appeared similar, but they were loose. Luckily, the Elves left us alone with the promise of coming back soon. The bit of tingle that came after they closed the door, left little doubt in my mind that they'd used a bit of magic to seal us in.

Harris leaned against the table. "What's your take on this, Lucas?"

"I'm not thrilled." I walked along the walls but didn't find anything else that looked like a window or door. We were effectively trapped in the room. "I get the point of not trusting the strangers. Can't say as I would do any different."

"Right." Harris nodded.

Vash sat on the table, the orange sparks cascading down from her hair were a little more diluted than normal. "You didn't not trust me when we first met."

I couldn't help but smile as I leaned against the wall. "You're a little different, Vash. I didn't have much choice, and you're special."

"Aren't Elves special too?" She cocked her head and ran her hand through her hair, throwing more sparks on the table.

"They don't appear as defenseless as you do." Even as the words came out, I knew they were silly. Vash was far from defenseless. Her power wasn't limitless, but she had a lot of umph when push came to shove.

"But don't you say appearances can be deceiving?" Vash laughed.

"She's right." Harris leaned his staff against the table.

"I know." Was I going to have to get used to her tossing my words back at me? There were so many things I didn't know about raising kids, and I doubted there was anyone out there who could give me hints about raising a Djinn kid. How many people just saw a Djinn as a way to get wishes? I knew she was more and was determined to give her the chance at a real life that her previous bearers hadn't. If people had treated her like a real person, she'd be older in her physical form, since Djinn only aged when they were outside their bonded item. For the past two thousand years, she'd only been out for the equivalent of eight years.

"We already know the Effrits are up to something, and now we have Dark Elves thrown into the mix. I don't doubt that there might be trouble heading toward Earth. If we can cut it off before it gets there, we need to. I don't like being trapped." I tapped on the wall. It sounded less than hollow. "I also don't like not having all the intel. They're keeping things from us."

"Yeah, I don't doubt that," Harris agreed. "But we wouldn't tell them everything either."

"No."

Before we could continue, a bit of magic danced through the room and Yang'fard opened the door.

"The royals are ready." Yang'fard stopped just a step into the room.

"That was fast." I wasn't used to people in power being able to put together things like an assault on a rival encampment in a short time.

"We might be long-lived by your standards, but it doesn't mean we're slow." Yang'fard held the door open as Harris, Vash and I headed out.

"I like that." I waited for Vash to clear the door behind Harris. "Doesn't always work that way on Earth."

"Then I'm glad we aren't on Earth." Yang'fard walked past us and led the way across the limb and toward the lift that would take us back to the throne room. "You humans can be very confusing."

The lift showed up, and we got on. The scent of lavender was heavier than it had been earlier. It helped cover up the blood smell that had permeated the area after the battle. I wrinkled my nose, wishing they had used something that wasn't so floral. At least my wolf didn't react to lavender the way he did to blood.

At the throne-room branch, we stepped off the lift and walked toward the doors where the wounded guards had been replaced with fresh ones or at least ones who'd had a chance to clean up after the battle. The door was open.

"You cannot stop me!" Yas'Fe'el shouted.

"You do not belong on the front line," An'Fa'el's voice was lower, and I would've missed the words if my ears had still been just human.

"Since when is your power equal to mine?" Yas'Fe'el responded. "You don't have the magic to keep yourself safe, let alone fight alongside our armies."

We walked into the room and the king made a cutting motion and stopped glaring as he turned toward us. "Thank you for staying to help us."

I rolled my eyes. "Not much choice. We want to stop this threat too. I take it you have a plan."

"We do." Yas'Fe'el stomped over to the small table that was sitting in front of their thrones. She gestured over it and light danced across the wooden surface. The light coalesced into a map. It was unlike anything I'd seen before, almost like something out of a science fiction movie. Lines that I suspected were the boundaries of the realms we'd traveled through appeared first, then features like rivers and mountains solidified.

"With the portal network shut down, there are only a few routes any of us can take to connect with the rest of the army." She ran a finger over the map, and lights appeared. "This is where we are going. We need to hit them fast. We aren't going to tolerate them assaulting us like this."

The map had a lot of different things that I couldn't identify. The thing was a bit different from the maps I used in the army, and the ones I grew up with around the ranch. It might have been the lights, but I could swear shadows moved over the map like living things.

"Where are we going?" I studied the lights.

"If we can reach it, to their fortress—" she traced a finger on a spot toward the edge of the map. "—it's not as fortified as they think. We strike them hard and fast. With the damage they've caused here they won't be expecting us. And with the portals shut down they won't know we're coming. We need to do as much damage as possible. "

Harris held up a hand. "If it's not TMI, how did you manage to shut down the portals? Individual mages can create portals between realms on their own."

Yas'Fe'el nodded. "That is correct, but we do have a certain level of control over the barriers between the realms we control. It wasn't easy to do, but we hardened the barriers to the point that no portal spells that we don't specifically allow can be created."

I pointed at the map. "Realms you control. That means anywhere you don't control hasn't been blocked. The Hun'se lands. There they can still create portals within their areas."

"Yes." She inclined her head sharply.

"What's to stop them from pulling the same stunt on us once we start our attack on their territory?" The shadows on the map grew darker. It wasn't just some kind of trick of light. Something was happening, maybe the map had a form of sympathetic magic that reflected the worlds it portrayed, I wasn't sure, but the shadows spread and

I didn't know what would happen if we got trapped somewhere they held sway.

"We'll be too fast." The queen shook her head. "They won't be expecting us."

"It's foolish to count on that." I put my finger down where the shadows were the deepest. "I'm betting we're going here. If you can pull a spell, I bet they have the same spells or some kind of thing that's in the same family. We need a way out."

"The Fae don't always work the same way as humans do." The king leaned over the table. "My lady has a good plan. Some of our mages and I can disrupt things from here while she leads you into battle. Your forces will decimate theirs." He patted her on the back. "She has a great plan."

"Throw enough eggs at the wall until there's sludge sliding down it? Can you even open portals in their realms now?" The more I heard the less I liked going in there without all of our allies and a ton of magical bullets.

"Yes." Yas'Fe'el straightened and stared me in the eye. "We sent a scouting party through before closing the network and sending Yang'fard to retrieve you. There wasn't anything standing in their way."

"So you sent troops through with no way back? Man, I hope you Elves are sturdier than you look." I'd seen similar operations in the army. Most of them didn't work out well for the scouts. If we were lucky, back then, they'd at least have a few rangers to back them up. Somehow, I doubted the Elves had thought of that.

"We are." The queen straightened as a young

Elf in a torn tabard ran forward.

She bowed low. "The army is assembled, your highnesses. They await you at the base of the tree."

A hard mask formed on the queen's face. "Then we're ready. An, you know what you must do."

The king's face was set in a similar hardness. "Please, be careful. We lost our daughter this day. I don't want to lose you too." He cast a glance at Vash, then turned and slumped up the steps to his throne and took his seat.

Yas'Fe'el nodded and turned toward the door. "Come."

Vash took my hand again.

Harris tapped his staff on the wooden floor three times like it was for luck or something. We followed the Elven queen from the throne room and toward the lift that would take us down to the waiting army.

18

Passing through the barriers that separated the various realms of Faerie was reminiscent of stepping into a portal. The landing wasn't as jarring as going through a portal. The barrier itself was little more than a glowing wall that ran from the green grass to the formless gray sky.

When we reached it, Yas'Fe'el put a hand on it and muttered something too faint to be heard. Then the barrier rippled, like a still pond after a rock has broken its surface. There wasn't any color change like when a portal opened. It was just ripples that slowly opened onto another realm.

Yang'fard and Slyl'fard were the first ones through. Like any good guards, they made sure things were safe before their queen walked through the door.

Beyond the barrier, a twisted forest of thorns waited for us. A narrow path wound through the dark gray plants. The thorns themselves were long and dangerous. Anyone thrown against them would be hurt like hell. If they were unlucky enough to get caught in something important, like a heart or lung, they could be killed. It reminded me of wild roses on steroids with fewer leaves and no flowers.

After several miles, we reached an open patch of ground. Yang'fard waved for us all to stop.

"I thought others were meeting us here." Yas'Fe'el looked around. Then stopped. "Ah, there they are."

I followed her gaze and blinked as some of the thorns separated from the dried vines and stepped forward. There were easily fifty of them suddenly walking toward us. They varied in size. Some towered over me, and others were rather stunted, coming just past my waist. They looked like dried, twisted trees, with thorn-like spines sticking out of their heads where their hair would've been. There were also longer thorns coming off their arms, and their fingers were long, sharp dagger-like appendages. They didn't carry any visible weapons, but we were in Faerie, and I knew there were lots of things that could be more dangerous than simple weapons. We were effectively surrounded, but we outnumbered them three to one. Reflex took over and my hand rested on Stormbringer.

Around us, none of the other warriors acted like they were on edge, beyond the general feeling of slowly building excitement as an army marched on toward its goal. I took a slow breath and tried to force my own edge down.

One of the larger thorn creatures walked up to Yas'Fe'el and knelt. "The Spiknards answer the call. We offer our thorns in service of the Fae. The ancient pact continues." His voice was like a dry wind rustling through the fall leaves.

Yas'Fe'el touched his shoulder. "I thank you for answering our call, Lord Rosonthorn."

"The Spiknards will always answer when the Lum'se'el call."

"And we appreciate that." Yas'Fe'el motioned for him to stand. "Should you ever have need of our swords, we will honor our pact as well."

It felt and sounded very formal, and I was a little surprised how much a foreign group of people could act and sound like dignitaries out of an old book.

Within minutes, we continued down another narrow path that cut through the dangerous forest. The Spiknards fell in behind the rest of the army as Yang'fard led us across the realm. There was just enough room for two people abreast without catching our gear on the thorns that reached out and seemed eager for any blood they could extract from unwary passersby.

Vash tugged on my hand. "Lucas, can you feel the eyes?"

"The eyes?" I looked around. "Do you think there's people watching us?"

She nodded. "All around us. Like there's people hiding in the vines."

"Is there magic?" With all the various Fae we were marching with, I couldn't help but feel like everyone was watching us. Even among them, we stood out. There wasn't another werewolf, or human, or Djinn. We stood out, and they were all watching us out of the corners of their eyes.

"Yes, but that's not how they're watching us."

"If they're right, how the portals are shut down, I doubt the Dark Elves are the ones watching," Harris kept his voice low like he was trying to keep the Fae around us from hearing. "But there could be their agents in all the realms. The portals might be shut down, but communications could still be open."

And where there were communications, people would know we were coming. There was too much at stake for us to not be hidden from the enemy.

I hurried over to Yas'Fe'el. "Your majesty. We're being watched."

She didn't break her stride. "I suspected."

"We should stop them before they can relay any of their information to their superiors." I'd taken out more than a few similar groups of insurgents over the years.

"Do you have an idea on how to deal with this, Mr. Lucas?" She still didn't stop.

There was so much I didn't know about the Fae, but I suddenly had a chance to do something beyond just marching with the army. "Maybe. We can take a small force and deal with them."

"Okay. Slyl'fard can pick a couple of warriors who can go with you." She glanced back at the army behind us. "You can leave your mage and Djinn with us."

My wolf uncoiled and growled.

The way the queen looked at me, I wondered if she'd heard him. Her eyes tightened for a moment.

"Harris can stay with you, but I'll take Vash with me. She is more sensitive to magic than I am." I wasn't about to leave Vash with her. Although the queen seemed welcoming to her, and Vash was her granddaughter, I didn't totally trust her. The way Yang'fard had reacted at first to seeing Vash, I didn't like the idea of leaving her with them, even if

Harris would be there too. With her at my side, I could protect her better.

"That skill could be useful." Yas'Fe'el nodded and gestured to Yang'fard.

The warrior slowed to walk next to us. "Yes, my queen."

"I want you to select a couple of warriors to go with Mr. Lucas to stop those who are observing us." Still, her steps never slowed.

"Ah, yes." Yang'fard nodded. "I wasn't sure if it was a problem."

"We need to make sure no one knows where we are." Yas'Fe'el glanced around. "So deal with them."

"I know the men." Yang'fard looked at me. "Come on, Lucas, we don't want to fall behind."

I nodded. "Of course." I glanced at Vash, still walking next to Harris. "Let's go, Vash. Harris, we'll catch up." I wanted to say something about keeping his eyes open, about not trusting the Elves, but he was just human and if I tried, they would hear. The Elves might appear to be our allies, for the moment, however, I wasn't ready to totally trust them.

From the look in his eyes, he understood. "Happy hunting."

"Thanks." I thumped him on the shoulder. I wasn't keen on leaving him with the Fae, but he was a grown mage, he should be able to handle it. The thing was, it felt like leaving part of my unit behind.

"Come on, Lucas," Yang'fard said behind me.

Two of the Spiknards hurried toward us.

"We're here to help." The shorter one thumped

his chest.

Yang'fard nodded. "This is your realm, your help is appreciated." He made a simple gesture and the familiar tingle of magic danced over us. "We should be undetectable until we strike."

It made sense that if we were dealing with magic, we were going to need to use some to help level the field.

"We won't be able to be seen." Vash laughed. "Let me help with being silent too. Sometimes unseen isn't enough." She added her own magic to Yang'fard's. It amazed me that I was getting more and more sensitive to it. Less than six months earlier, I wouldn't have noticed or believed in magic.

A couple of other Elves came over like they could see us, and without another word, we trudged off from the bulk of the army. Then we disappeared into the thorns with the Spiknards leading the way.

The Spiknards knew paths that were nearly impossible to spot. Most of the thorns seemed to move away from us like they were conscious of us and our placement among them. A couple of times, I glanced back and watched the pathway close behind us. It was incredible, and not something I would've ever seen on Earth.

"They're over there." Vash pointed to our left.

We paused and stared. I couldn't see anything. I sniffed, letting my wolf side peek out. The various scents of the thorn forest hit me. The dry wood.

Dusty gray soil. A breeze that could've been in Afghanistan rattled through the thorns. A soft floral fragrance drifted to me. It held a note of musk. Unless there were flowers we couldn't see, it was out of place.

One of the Spiknards looked up and snarled. "Blumea."

The other Spiknard nodded and then stepped into the vines, disappearing from us as he melded into the bark.

Yang'fard motioned for the rest of us to stay still.

The floral scent grew stronger.

A nearby vine shook violently. The Spiknard who'd disappeared tumbled out of a vine with a smaller plant creature in its grasp. Two more similar plant creatures rolled out with it.

"Take them." Yang'fard raised his sword and rushed forward.

I whipped out Stormbringer, targeted, and fired. It was just a regular bullet. I was saving the magical ones for when they would be needed. It caught a Blumea in the center of its green forehead. Thin green sap sprayed out as it crumpled across the Spiknard the others were attacking.

An intense wave of the floral scent hit just before all the vines around us started to shake.

Growling, I looked for another target as Yang'fard and one of the other Elves took out the other two diminutive plant Fae.

"There." Vash pointed, then whipped her finger around in a tight circle several times.

Wind lashed out from her hand, blasting a trio

of Blumea into the thick thorns of the vines they'd emerged from. High-pitched screams rattled from their throats as they died.

I targeted a couple more and squeezed off shots. When I stopped and thought about it, I didn't know if they were the good guys or the bad guys, just that they'd attacked our unit. They weren't acting like the good guys. Again, I wished I had a Fae playbook so I could stay up to speed.

A loud series of pops and cracks from the vines sounded like they came from all around us. I jerked around as bark and twigs showered us. More Blumea burst out and swarmed similar to the way the Sprites had attacked back on Earth.

Several of them came straight at me, using the force of their exiting the vines to carry them across the tight space like little vegetative projectiles.

Vash shouted.

I stumbled under the assault. My wolf roared up unbidden. I couldn't stop him. The change was unlike the ones I'd endured on recent full moons with my werewolf mentor Chad Kilkari. It was sudden. The pain was just a flash that vanished as my wolf struggled to get out of my clothes that had been mostly shredded.

Unlike with the Sprites, nothing stopped the change. We dropped to four paws and snapped at the Blumea who stabbed us with diminutive thorns that were just long enough to get through our fur. Weird sap filled our mouth as we chomped down on a small Fae.

Next to me, Vash blasted another couple of Blumea into thorns and bits of bark.

Elven swords flashed and trimmed more Blumea out of the fight.

The wolf took over, scratching away two plant Fae. We jerked to the side, snapping at two Blumea yanking on our tail. Each tug sent stabs of pain through us. They might've been smaller than us, but they made up for it in numbers. The vines continued to crack and pop, spitting more and more Blumea out into the fray.

Wind danced around us.

Vash shouted again and her winds tore across the battlefield. More Blumea flew onto the thorns surrounding us. Some of them screamed; others fell without a sound.

We snapped and clawed at the waves of attackers. They went down easily, but there were so many of them. The wolf knew instinctively how to handle them. Like a beast fighting mosquitos, we spun, clawed, and snapped. They fell and lay on the ground.

The Elves and Spiknards fought, leaving many bodies lying around as we did.

After several minutes, the popping and cracking stopped. No more Blumea appeared.

One of the Elven warriors lay still on the ground, dead Blumea had stabbed him in the eyes. His blood mingled with their sap.

Yang'fard looked at us. "Wolf. It's over. Turn back."

We growled, still bristled from the fight. Our need to spill blood raged. Muscles tightened as we prepared to spring on the warrior.

Vash's soft singing voice danced through us.

"Lucas, come back to me. Wolf, you did a good job protecting me." She stroked our head. "You can let Lucas back in control."

Her magic washed over us.

We licked her hand. Then the wolf turned and retreated to the depths of my soul where he spent his time when he wasn't merging with my body. The pain of the transformation engulfed me.

Moments later, I was sitting on the ground panting.

With a soft smile, Vash stroked my sweaty hair. "You did good."

I returned her smile and ruffled her hair. "So did you."

A soft breeze danced over my skin, reminding me that my clothes didn't survive a shift. It was going to suck having to either borrow Elven clothes that would probably be way too tight for my muscular frame or spending our assault on the Dark Fae naked. At least my hiking boots lay a few feet away next to Stormbringer and my magical sword. I wouldn't be barefoot.

"Here. I can help with your clothes." Vash sounded like she could read my thoughts. She did that from time to time, and I was getting used to it.

"I didn't think your magic lasted more than a day." I gathered up my shredded shirt and cargo pants.

"Then I'll redo it in the morning if we're still here." Vash smiled and waved her hand. Magic washed over my hands, sending tingles around my hands and up my arms. If felt like I was about to touch an electric fence, then it was over, and my clothes were back together. Everything was the way it had been when the fight started.

"Djinn magic is handy." Yang'fard looked down at us.

"Thank you." Vash glanced at him.

I stood and put the pants on first, getting dressed before looking further at the dead lying around. The two Spiknards were rubbing rags over their fingers and other thorns. It reminded me of cleaning a gun, or sword. Soldiers might be different in size, shape, and color, but they were still soldiers. I understood their actions, and the familiarity of them helped me feel more at home, as much as losing control to the wolf gnawed at me. Sometimes grounding helped me not dwell on my own situation.

Little Blumea littered the ground and hung from thorns, some still oozed sap that dripped to the ground with tiny plops. They looked like wilted flower dolls dangling from a barbed-wire fence.

The other Elf wrapped a cloth around a deep scratch on his right forearm and had several nasty marks on his face and neck where Blumea had scored hits. The little Fae had been relentless in their attacks. It made sense that they would know how to use their size to their advantage. Small and mighty.

"We should return to the queen." Yang'fard finished wiping his sword and slipped it back in its scabbard. "I can't feel any more of them around. We can only hope they haven't had time to pass the information on to their Dark-Elf allies."

Not knowing how easily the Fae could communicate across the realms, I could only shrug as I tied my shoes and straightened, trying to be ready for whatever was going to happen. If there was one thing I understood, it was that the unexpected was to be expected, particularly when it came to battles. It was another thing that was true no matter if I was on Earth, or in Faerie.

Yang'fard barely glanced at the downed Elf, as he turned to head back the way we'd come. We were at war. Only after the war would we have time to mourn the dead, and sometimes, like when the army was marching away, there wasn't even time to properly lay them to rest. Maybe Elves didn't bury their dead. I didn't know, but it felt cold to just walk away and leave a fallen member of our temporary unit lying there on the ground for the earth under him to reclaim.

19

Two realms later, we marched on toward the final barrier before we entered areas controlled by the Hun'se. The place was like some kind of giant stinking bog. I wrinkled my nose as a steaming mud bubble exploded in a rush of noxious gas. In the distance, volcanoes spewed fire and lava into the sky, casting enough smoke to make the whole area hazy, grimy, and hot. Tall, withered trees full of hanging moss shrouded everything. Everything about the place made me nervous. I hated not being able to see everything around me.

The column of Elves, Spiknards, and other Fae moved faster than I expected them to. It made me wonder if the queen or one of the others was using a bit of magic to help us make good time. If they were, it was something so subtle that I couldn't feel anything.

"This isn't what I would expect a Faerie realm to be like." Harris paced alongside me, his staff making no sound whatsoever as he put it down with each step. "Even the thorn forest was something I could've envisioned."

I nodded. "Makes you wonder what the natives are like."

"You do know that some of the realms don't have creatures living in them." Yang'fard walked on my other side. "Faerie is ever-changing, and we who live here change with it."

His words made me laugh. "Every world changes and all people evolve as their environments do."

Yang'fard shook his head. "Not everyone does. Some species are incapable of change, and they are swept away by the tides of time."

"So some things hold true no matter what realm we are in." I glanced down at Vash. She was in some ways ancient and others just a kid. In the months I'd been her guardian, she'd been quick to pick up on new things. I wasn't used to kids, so I had no idea how fast normal kids adapted to stuff, but I was proud of how she seemed so eager to take things in.

"They do," Harris agreed as another of the mud bubbles exploded spilling foul-smelling gas over us again.

I was going to be so happy to get out of the swamp to somewhere that hopefully had a more fragrant aroma. So far, I hadn't seen any rhyme or reason to how the Elven realms worked as far as their individual biomes went. We'd traversed stony lands, the thorn forest, a foggy land where we couldn't see more than a few feet. A couple of verdant valleys had been a pleasant change from some of the other areas.

A shout rose from the back of the line.

I turned toward the shout.

Steel on steel rang out along with more

shouting.

Pulling Stormbringer, I took a step toward the sound, then glanced down at Vash. "Stay with Harris."

She put her hands on her hips. "I can help."

"I'd rather you stay here."

The yelling got closer and closer. I wanted to at least try to keep the danger away.

"Look out." Vash gestured and magic shot up around the two of us.

An Elf, in the murky armor of the Dark Elves, swung his sword at me, but her shield blocked the blow, knocking him a couple of feet as the force of his own blow rebounded on him. I leveled my handgun at his head and squeezed the trigger.

He tried to block the bullet but was too slow. I caught him in the temple and spun him around. Before he crashed to the ground, another Dark Elf appeared, striding over him and striking the shield. His blows didn't do anything.

Vash stood strong and safe.

"Harris, get over here." I fired again as a Dark Elf rushed him. I didn't know if his magic was strong enough to deflect something like a sword.

Harris swung his staff and blocked a blow from another Elf that came out of nowhere. They were just rising out of the swamp, like the reek and heat of the mud didn't affect them. A bit of magic drew my attention. Elves were appearing out of thin air. If the barriers between the realms were really locked, then they had to be making their portals *within* the realm, if that was even possible,

With another swing, Harris knocked his

assailant on his butt. Then he ran back toward us.

I fired at two more Elves as they tried to attack him. One blocked the bullet with his sword. The other shot found a home in an Elven shoulder. I'd bought Harris enough time to reach Vash's protection.

She dropped the shield long enough for him to stumble in.

The queen shouted something that didn't translate, then magic lashed out across the growing battlefield.

Vash grunted and stumbled at the power swept over us.

Around us, others dropped to the ground, friend and foe alike.

"Hang in there, Vash." Harris put his hand on her shoulder and a soft glow radiated from him to her.

I wondered if it was something he could teach me. If I could help her with magic when he wasn't around, that might be a good thing.

Another magical shout rang out from the back of the vanguard of Light Elves. Power rolled out like it was someone reflecting Yas'Fe'el's spell. Some of those who had managed to ride out her spell went down on the second wave. Only a few Fae remained on their feet, although around us, the ones who went down under the first wave were standing.

Harris dropped to his knees, holding his head. "Damn, that's harsh."

"What can we do?" I switched out my clip, I'd gone through so many bullets that, if I started shooting again, I'd run out quickly.

"Just keep shooting." Harris sat down. "Sorry, Vash, I don't have enough power to keep you going."

She patted his head. "It's okay." Her sparks, that had dimmed, were nearly back to normal brightness.

A bright light came from the end of the line as more Elves appeared out of thin air. Seconds later, a fireball streaked overhead. The queen bounced it off, sending it flying into the swamp where it exploded, setting the swamp on fire.

I stared through the vanguard who were struggling back to their feet. There was a Dark Elf back there who wasn't in the same armor as the warriors. He stood there with a staff and a robe. Squeezing off another shot with the new bullets, I hoped I was right.

Stormbringer thundered over the fire's crackling. My own fireball soared across the battlefield. It bounced off an invisible barrier, but the Elf took a couple of steps backward. I fired again, squeezing three shots in tight succession. The third shot got through. The mage crumpled.

Another gunshot rang out. It didn't sound like it was magically enhanced.

A wolf howled.

Chills ran through me. I needed to run.

"Lucas." Vash clutched my hand. "Lucas, look at me."

The howl didn't repeat. Even as sweat soaked my back. We were in the middle of an Elven battle. I couldn't lose it. I had to hold it together.

With a deep breath, I looked at Vash. "I'm

going to be okay." Deep inside me, my wolf uncoiled. The need to protect Vash fought with the urge to run, but between the wolf and Vash, I held it together, at least for that one howl.

"Whaaahooo!" a human shouted somewhere nearby.

"How is there a human here?" I glanced at Harris, still sitting on the ground.

He shrugged, then closed his eyes. "There's more mages than just me around. I can't answer that." He already sounded tired and the fight was just really starting.

More gunshots rang out.

I looked up and stared. A huge green Fae, two-handed swinging a staff and sword, ran through the troops that were jumping to their feet. At his side, the biggest, meanest-looking wolf I'd ever seen leaped to the back of a Fae who was trying to rise. But what stopped me was the man riding the back of the Fae, like a child riding on the back of its father.

"Santiago?" I looked at the man on the Fae. How was Theo Santiago in Faerie? And, what was he doing riding a huge green Fae what was nearly as tall as two men?

A Dark Elf popped out of thin air and jumped toward them, with its sword raised.

Before the strike could land, I caught the Elf in the chest with a fireball bullet. He exploded.

As the battle raged, I tried to mow down as many Dark Elves as I could. They went down as easily to Santiago's non-magical bullets as they did to my fireball ones. The Dark Elves didn't stand a chance.

Then Santiago shot one of the Lum'se'el. With the differences in armor, there was no way to miss that the next Elf that fell to his bullets wasn't the same as a Dark Elf.

We weren't in Afghanistan, where friends and foes often looked the same. I couldn't let one friend take out an ally. It wasn't in me. "Santiago, stop!"

Running through Vash's shield, I rushed toward him as fast as I could. There was the briefest tingle as I passed her magic, then the overlying magic of the battlefield danced across my skin. It was like running down a fence line with my hand on the live wire set on high. My wolf growled and lent me the agility to almost dance through the warriors who were rising to resume their battle. Swords passed over my head and missed my arms as I wove a path through them. I had to get to Santiago and see about turning his bullets to our side.

"Santiago, don't shoot the ones with brighter armor!" I skidded to a stop and stared up at the huge plant Fae he was riding. Why was he riding the giant green man?

"Lucas?" Santiago stared down at me.

"What are you doing here?" He asked the same time I did.

The wolf striding next to the giant leaped past me, bringing a Dark Elf down. "A battlefield isn't the place to have a chat."

"What?" I turned and stared as the wolf raise bloody jowls and stared at me.

"Use your wolf." The wolf stared at me as if he could see through me. Then he looked up at Santiago. "I told you he was a wolf and you didn't believe me." Like other Fae, he knew what I was. Maybe it made a kind of sense that Fae wolves could speak.

"Bullets are better than claws and fangs." I fired at another Dark Fae rushing toward them. Theo fired as well. The Elf went down. I wasn't up to debating things with a wolf, particularly in the middle of a major fight.

"Always use what you have." Snarling, the wolf launched at another Elf.

The huge Fae swung his massive sword, cleaving a Dark Elf in half. "Less talk, more fighting." Its words were in English and didn't need the translating spell, although he did have a bit of an English accent.

"Set me down." Theo tapped the huge Fae on the shoulder, then shot another Elf who charged toward us.

I popped an Elf that appeared behind the big plant guy. "Get over there." I pointed to where Vash and Harris were behind her shield.

Theo landed uncomfortably, as the Fae handed him the staff that was darkened with Elf blood. "Here, Theo." Taking the staff, he leaned on it and looked uncomfortable.

"What happened?" I offered Theo my off-hand for a bit of balance, which he was lacking.

"Bad landing." Theo hobbled as we headed toward Vash.

I shot again, and Stormbringer clicked with an empty magazine.

"Here." Theo fired for me, taking down an Elf who rose from the ones who'd been knocked down by the queen's magic.

Popping out the empty magazine, I switched back to regular bullets. It made sense to save the special shot for an opponent who needed them. I slammed the magazine home, just in time to bring up Stormbringer and take out another Elf who was part of a group of five swarming us.

The big Fae hacked away with his sword, while Theo and I took out two and the wolf brought one down.

Vash screamed.

I turned from Theo, nearly dropping him in the mud. A large group of Fae covered her shield. It had collapsed under their assault. Winds lashed out, blowing some of them away, but there were too many of them.

It made sense to fire toward them, but I worried that I might miss a shot and hit her or Harris. "Vash!" My wolf roared forward and we let Theo fall as we leaped into the fray. In the close quarters, the fangs and claws made sense. As a wolf, I could tell if I was hitting them or something else. It was the fastest, least-painful change I'd had.

Our claws slid off Dark Elf armor, trying to find purchase even as they fell back. Then at the edge of the armor, we found something soft. We tore into it, ripping the armor away and giving us access to the flesh underneath. Elf blood sprayed around us. We kept up the assault.

Next to us, the other wolf tore into another Elf.

Gunfire sounded from behind us.

The huge green Fae's shouts rang out.

Wind and lightning lashed the moist ground.

More fire erupted around us.

Another Elf went down under our fangs and claws.

A sword bit into our flank. We spun and grabbed the warrior's throat in our teeth.

Hot blood flooded our mouth.

I gagged and recoiled. There was something different in tearing out the throat of a humanoid and taking down a deer. Something in the taste was strange and made it all the more real.

My wolf took total control, shoving my recoil and me away. For the first time in months, he was all there was. I was just an observer as he protected Vash. With the strange Fae wolf at his side, he ignored blows that would've left me staggering and in acute pain.

Even the Fae wolf's howls didn't affect me. I, David Lucas, was too far gone.

After several minutes, with magic and swords blazing around us, the sounds of battle died down. I tried to reach out, but the wolf wanted to stay in control.

"Lucas?" Vash ran her fingers through our fur. Small, delicate sparks danced around us. Her voice, like always, reached down past the fur and found my human skin. Somehow she reached beyond the wolf, and touched not a paw but a hand and pulled me out of the fur.

With a whine, my wolf retreated to the depths of my soul, where he lay down, with his head on his paws, watching, waiting until the next time Vash would be in danger, and our human side wouldn't be enough to keep her safe. He'd done a great job, and a sense of satisfaction flowed out of him, overriding my sense of uselessness.

20

Shaking, I uncurled from the pain of the shift back to human. Although the other werewolves told me the pain would subdue in time, so far, I hadn't felt that. As the pain subdued, the silence surprised me. There were soft moans around us. Elves and other Fae were in pain, some were dying.

"You are indeed a great warrior." Queen Yas'Fe'el stood a few feet from me. "No one else slew as many Hun'se as you did today. You deserve armor worthy of your power." Magic danced over me as she touched my shoulder. Unlike when Vash had rebuilt my clothes the last time I shifted, it was stronger magic. She was drawing something around me. Yang'fard's words about Elves building things reverberated through me as power engulfed me.

When it faded, I glanced at my arms and torso. Silver chain mail, almost the same color as my fur glistened there, but there wasn't the burning that happened the couple of times I'd touched silver since the attack. Maybe Elven magic made it something different, or just had a way of protecting me from the effects. On my chest was a blue wolf head. From the weight on my head, there was some kind of armor there too.

"That's great." Harris stayed on the ground next to Vash. "Elven armor is legendary."

"We believe in rewarding valor in our service, mage." Yas'Fe'el smiled softly.

"Is that what it was?" I glanced at Vash. "Are you okay?"

She sighed. For the first time since I'd met her, there weren't any sparks flowing around her when she wasn't using her magic to hide them. "Tired."

The fact that she hadn't retreated to the bell told me she'd not totally exhausted herself. "This round of the battle is over. Rest."

"We will stay here for a little while, and get our bearings." Yas'Fe'el glanced around. "And heal our wounded before we go on." Her gaze found Santiago and she knelt next to him. "You arrived with Vaern, human warrior."

"Sergeant Theo Santiago, your majesty." Santiago leaned on his staff, sweat ran down his face, smearing mud and blood.

"You are wounded, Sergeant." The queen smiled softly. "I will send my healer to you. We need every sword and bullet possible in the coming fight. Or battle has only just begun." Then she rose and continued to inspect the other wounded.

Santiago stared as she walked away. "She's the queen? Where's the king?"

"Back at the World Tree." I went back to where I'd shifted. Stormbringer and its holster lay on the damp ground. My sword was just a couple of feet away. I hurried over to them, fastening my gun belt on before slipping the sword, still in its scabbard across my shoulder. With my new armor, I wasn't as flexible as I was in my normal clothes. Drawing the sword would be awkward. It was too long to easily strap to my waist opposite my handgun where drawing would be easier. I wondered how anyone ever managed to use swords in things like plate armor. Maybe I needed to talk to one of the Elven warriors for some pointers.

"That's some sword, Lucas." Santiago was still leaning on his staff like he couldn't put any weight on his right leg.

"Yeah. I can even use it… a bit." After Garnet Godfree had spent weeks trying to teach me to swing it with a bit of accuracy.

"Is it better than a gun?" Santiago slipped his sidearm into its holster.

I shook my head. "Not that I've noticed, but something tells me that there might be things like Dragons where it will be."

Santiago pointed at me. "Wait, there's Dragons?"

With a laugh, I nodded. "Yeah, there're Dragons. Nasty critters."

"Worf, did you know there were Dragons?" Santiago looked at the wolf.

I stared at him too. That was the same name as his support dog from our group meeting. With everything going on, I shouldn't be surprised that the dog had a disguise like Vash used to hide her sparks and other unusual features.

The big wolf shrugged. "Theo, I know what you know."

"Santiago, how did you get here?" I wanted to know, and I wasn't sure we were in the right place to talk about it.

"Fell through a portal." He glanced around and stared for a moment at the retreating queen. After a slight frown, he looked at me. "Not the first time. How about you?"

"First time." It definitely wasn't the place or time to be telling our origin stories.

"Wolf." Yang'fard drew my attention. "We could use a hand with the wounded."

I nodded. "Yeah, we've got wounded of our own." I nodded toward Santiago. "The queen said, Santiago would get a healer."

"Working on it." Yang'fard sighed. "We weren't ready for a battle at this point. Beyond the next portal will be the last set of reinforcements."

"So this worked out for them." I waved toward the Dark Elves I'd taken out while in wolf form. When I looked at them, the taste of their blood ran through my mouth and I forced the bile that rose in my throat back. It was one thing to kill a man with a gun or a bomb, but tearing someone's throat out wasn't cool, although there was a sense of honor to it. Close-combat opponents had the chance to deal damage to one another, where snipers weren't in nearly as much risk as foot soldiers.

Yang'fard nodded. "Yes, it did. Now we need to regroup. We don't have time to fall back. It's forward, or nothing."

A chill went through me. I flashed back to being in the desert after the werewolf attack, when half the unit was down and we couldn't contact the base due to what I had begun to understand was probably magic working against us. My unit had changed,

Carson and the others were gone, replaced with Vash, Harris, and now Santiago and Worf. In a way, Yang'fard and the other Fae were also part of it. Again we were cut off with only ourselves to fall back on. I wasn't going to lose another unit.

"Let's get everyone patched up." I glanced at Santiago, Vash, and Harris sitting there with Worf standing, ears up, tail out, and ready to tear anyone who came near them apart. "Harris, can you and Vash keep things held down here?"

Harris lay his staff across his legs. "Yeah. I got it here."

"Thanks." I gave him a thumbs up and followed Yang'fard to the area where more of the Lum'se'el were wounded than the Dark Elves.

Watching the Elven healers work, a new appreciation for magic welled up in me. Sure, I'd felt Vash's power, but she hadn't used it to mend broken flesh and bones. As far as I knew, none of the magic users around me had the ability to heal.

I made it back to where Vash was standing. The orange sparks from her hair were nearly back to normal.

She looked up at me and smiled. "We survived, and I didn't get forced back to my bell." She glanced around. "I feel stronger here. I don't know if I'm growing, or it's the innate magic of Faerie."

"I'm voting for a combination of the two." Harris stood using his staff. "You're growing but I agree, being in Faerie is invigorating."

Santiago leaned on his own staff but didn't look as unsteady as he had earlier. "The healing was amazing. I hate turning ankles like that."

"And if you weren't so clumsy on your two feet, you wouldn't get hurt so often." Worf had relaxed to sprawling between Vash and Santiago.

Harris looked at Santiago. "You have a magical glow. Do you know where it comes from?"

"These?" Santiago pulled a pair of wire-rimmed aviator sunglasses from his shirt pocket.

Holding out his hand, Harris offered to take them. "Maybe." He held them up and raised an eyebrow. "There's magic in them. They let you see Fae." He handed them back to Santiago. "But there more to it than that."

Santiago tucked them back in his pocket. "Like what?"

"Magic." Harris held out his hand and a bit of a glow filled it.

"No way." Santiago shook his head. "I can use the glasses. I've got Worf, but beyond that, I'm just a soldier. I'm just a regular human."

Cocking his head, Harris studied Santiago. "No, there's more. Maybe-"

"We need to keep moving." Queen Yas'Fe'el appeared where the front of the column had been. "Our living have been tended to. We must press the attack and hope they haven't had time to shore up their defenses." Behind her, a bubble of mud exploded, sending out a wave of reeking odor. It was like some kind of sour rallying cry about how screwed up things were at that moment. If we stayed there, we'd be stunk out and the Dark Elves would find us sitting there in the mud holding our noses.

Yang'fard stood at her shoulder. "The rear ranks are ready to move, my liege."

"Thank you, Yang'fard." The queen turned and marched to the front of the line.

I watched her go. There was a glow about her that scoured the blood and grime from her armor, making it spotless. Another useful thing magic could do, although I doubted the queen would share the technique with me, but maybe Vash would do it if things got bad.

"Guess we need to get moving." I held my hand out to Vash.

Vash took it, then put a hand out to Worf, running it through his fur. "Can I walk with Worf? He'll protect me."

"Sure." I smiled.

"She's too old to be your daughter," Santiago said softly as we fell into the line of the Fae army.

"How do you know?" Sure, Santiago and I had a history, and it had been years since we'd talked more than just a few words when we met at the group meeting. That meant we had more than a little bit of catching up to do.

Santiago shrugged. "Okay, maybe she isn't, but she looks nothing like you."

I laughed. "Yeah, she's not biologically mine. But I'm her guardian. Someone, something gave me her vessel and told me she liked me and asked me to take care of her. In some ways, she's a guide to this mixed-up world I've found myself in."

Looking at Worf, Santiago nodded. "We need guides sometimes. So how did you become a werewolf?"

That was a harder question to answer. I kept the answer simple and direct. "My unit was attacked by a pack while we were on patrol in Afghanistan. Then we got ambushed by some Effrits. I was the only one who survived."

Santiago nodded slowly. "That's close to what your file said."

I stared at him. "You read my file?" I knew there was a difference between my official records and the public ones. Publicly the supernatural world didn't exist.

"I take a moment and check out everyone who's been assigned to the support group. I don't dig deep, but I do enough to at least get a feel for what the new people have gone through."

It made perfect sense. In his situation as a group leader, I'd want to know about the people who were there.

"Do you really have PTSD?" Santiago sidestepped a divot in the trail where the swamp pressed toward us.

"Yeah." I nodded. "I have PTSD. I'm still sorting out living with it, and living with being a werewolf."

"It's not something you can just flip a switch and turn on and off." Santiago patted me on the shoulder. "By the way, I'm guessing the silver hair is due to your wolf. It looks good on you."

I'd gotten used to it, and Santiago was the first person from my past that I'd crossed paths with since. One thing I'd wondered about was how my family would react when I went up to Montana, or they came down to Colorado. Mom would probably freak, but I had already gotten a story of stress in battle causing it. It felt a little far-reaching, but it wasn't unheard of. Somehow, talking to Santiago about it felt good, like some kind of easy coming out.

"Thanks." Garnet, Cin, and some of the others had told me similar things. Coming from Santiago, it carried a little more weight.

Striding between two of the volcanoes, we reached the barrier between the realms. The air was filled with sulfur. I coughed, as did a bunch of the others. Even Worf was coughing by the time we were within touching distance. Vash was the only one not coughing. The queen touched the barrier and created a gateway so we could step from the fetid swamp into a much greener land beyond.

21

Rolling green hills that reminded me of the foothills in the Rockies were peppered with the trees that if they hadn't been light blue, could've been the familiar lodge-pole pines that covered those slopes. The going was easier than it had been through the swamp realm. There weren't any reeking pustules of mud exploding every few steps. Here and there were a few herds of grazers that looked like a cross between deer and miniature elephants with branched antlers coming out of their bulbous heads.

The group of Fae warriors, nearly as large as the vanguard we'd been marching with, waited for us. They were a collection of various species ranging from more diminutive Sprites than I'd ever seen, to towering giants that dwarfed even Santiago's friend, Vaern. If the force had been possible on Earth, it wasn't something I would've wanted to face. The power was too variable to be easily defended again. I wished I knew more about the Dark Elves and their allies, beyond the Effrits. The more knowledge I had, the better I could've planned for what was to come.

"Can't say as I ever thought I'd see something like this." Harris marched along, using his staff as a walking stick. "I mean this is incredible. Garnet is going to be mad she missed this."

He was right. I couldn't help but chuckle. "She *is* into her fantasy worlds, isn't she? I can't believe you guys know so much magic and haven't been here before."

"We know about things like the portals, but haven't done more than just step through from time to time to shut them down, then come back to Earth," Harris said. "We're protectors of our area. Most mages have been tasked with keeping things like Fae out of our world. They aren't part of the oath. They could cause a lot of trouble if they came through in large numbers."

"And even when they are just in ones and twos, they shouldn't be there," Santiago added, then dropped his voice. "That's where people like me come in."

Again, it wasn't the time or place to talk about things, so I didn't ask what had brought him to Faerie, beyond stumbling through a portal. I kept my questions to myself, and would until we were back on Earth. Maybe we could sit down over a few beers and really, truly get caught up.

Yang'fard dropped back from where he and Slyl'fard had been marching at the front of the column. "You should prepare yourselves. After the next barrier, we'll be in their domain. We don't know what to expect."

"Not even any hints?" I wanted intel, it was important for success.

"Maybe." Yang'fard fell into step with us. "Unfortunately, we aren't sure who will be with them. The Hun'se themselves are masters of magic, in some forms better than Lum'se'el. We deal in light. They deal in shadows. So far, you've seen their ability for short-range portals and one of their sorcerers cast a few spells to counter our queen. When we're on their home ground, their magic will be stronger. That's just the way magic works. Our hope is that our numbers will be enough."

"Any clue on how to make the most of our forces?" I glanced at Vash, remembering how she said she was stronger in Faerie.

"Not yet." Yang'fard looked uncomfortable. He shuffled his feet and put his hands behind his back. "Truthfully, it's been years since any of the light court have been to the Hun'se lands. There's lots of ways they could've changed. We may be nearly immortal and change comes slowly, but change happens to every species, even Elves."

Vash nodded. "Even the Djinn change."

Again, a shout rose up, this time from the front of the vanguard. We were closer to that and on a higher edge of the gentle slope. A host of Elves mounted on huge lizards came at us. Behind them rode Orcs mounted on similar beasts.

I pulled Stormbringer from his holster. The magazine was still loaded with regular bullets. They would work against the Elves, and the Orcs were magic resistant, if they were like the ones we'd fought before, so they would be better there too. Again, I wished I'd thought to bring more bullets. Without the power that Stormbringer brought to the field, I'd be left with the sword. I hoped I'd be good enough with it to make a dent in the battle to come.

The Lum'se'el guards swarmed around their queen while the rest of the warriors spread out in a line across the slope. With their swords and bows and arrows, they prepared to meet the enemy.

My unit took up a place just to the left of the queen. I wanted Vash safe but also wasn't about to hide in the thick of the warriors. The more hits we could score quickly, the better. Vaern lumbered to stand in front of us.

"Use me for cover, Theo, and friends." He looked down and grinned, exposing rows of barky teeth. "It takes more than a few Elves to damage me or my kind." He gestured down the line where other plant giants were wading toward the front of the Elves and others. More human-looking giants moved a short distance behind the line, pulling up boulders from under the ground and piling them around their feet.

The Elves rode toward us.

A boulder flew over our heads and hit the ground just shy of their lead riders.

They kept coming. Their lizard mounts easily navigating around the sudden obstacles that appeared as more giants threw boulders toward them. As far as useful in taking out the enemy, they weren't, but they did help slow them down as they had to veer about. The distraction caused by the change of course gave the archers on our side a chance to get some arrows off.

Hun'se fell from their mounts. Lizards that escaped the arrows kept coming. The Orcs shouted behind the Elves. More arrows flew.

I watched from the protection of Vaern's leg.

Tightening my grip on Stormbringer, I waited for the other warriors to get within range.

"They're getting closer." Santiago had his own gun out.

"Not close enough." Worf crouched near us, ready to jump into the fray. "Don't waste your bullets."

Santiago looked at me as he nodded. "He's got a good sense of distance."

"It's a wolf thing." I couldn't help smiling. "We've got really strong senses. Not to mention I was always a better shot than you were."

"An old woman with palsy is a better shot than Theo." Worf chuffed with his own laughter.

"At least I have thumbs, Mutt," Santiago retorted.

In all my dreams, I never thought I'd be going into battle with a smart-ass wolf, a Djinn, a mage, and all the various Fae. It was unreal, and I just hoped we all survived it.

"Fire at will," Worf commanded, as the thick hair along his spine stood straight and tall.

Around us, more arrows and boulders flew.

Then the flashes of magic started. The queen and her mages took down more of the attacking army.

I picked the largest Orc in the middle of their line and fired. Stormbringer roared and instead of falling, the Orc raised his shield and deflected my bullet.

Vash's hands glowed and her hair was almost totally engulfed in blue and white sparks as she thrust out her hands and lightning danced through the Hun'se. Her sparks dulled slightly, only to build again.

As the lightning hit, part of the line of attackers turned away from the queen and headed toward us. The Orcs roared louder.

A chill went through me. They were after us, not the Lum'se'el.

"Vash, stay close." I touched her shoulder.

My wolf pushed out through the depths of my soul. He wanted us to protect Vash.

We merged slightly, not all the way, where he'd be in control. I blinked and my vision tightened. The battlefield was in stark relief. The broad green foreheads of the Orcs were covered in the shiny glaze of sweat. Somehow that surprised me. It made them like us.

Pushing aside the similarities, I focused on them. If more of them blocked my shots, I was going to need all the luck I could muster. Two shots seconds apart. My target blocked the first one, but the second one hit home, catching him in the eye and knocking him from his mount. With as much steadiness as I could muster, I took out two more the same way. Beside me, Santiago's gun barked and more Orcs fell.

Harris put his staff down, and the ground beneath us rolled. Lizards, Elves, and Orcs stumbled, some going down.

I took advantage and brought down another couple before I ran out of bullets. I changed the magazine as fast as possible.

Vash got off another series of lightning strikes, then a dark smoke drifted along the ground, swirling past the pounding feet of humanoids and lizards, coming straight toward us.

It didn't act like anything remotely normal. There was something wrong with it. The hairs on my arm stood on end. "Vash! Look out."

The dark-haired Djinn who'd kidnapped Vash months earlier materialized from the smoke. It slowly coalesced from smoke to flesh. His long beard and hair were the last parts to solidify. He pointed at me, and magic slammed into me, throwing me backward.

"Lucas!" Vash ran toward me and something stopped her.

"No, little one." The Djinn's words were perfect English and loud enough to carry over the sounds of battle. "You're mine."

Vash pounded against the barrier that held her at bay.

My wolf surged.

"Stop." I pleaded. *"We're going to need thumbs for this."*

For the first time ever, he pressed inside me, molding himself to my skin as opposed to taking me over. His strength flooded through me, along with his agility and speed.

I fired off a couple of rounds, and he blocked them like they were nothing. "Back off. You're not getting her."

"Do you think you have it in you, wolf?" He sneered.

A deep growl rumbled out of our throat.

He flicked his hand and power roared toward me.

"No!" Harris thrust his staff toward me and the Djinn's spell rebounded, catching him in the chin.

The Djinn stumbled back a couple of steps and shook his head.

Vash shoved her hands out and shattered the barrier holding her prisoner.

Santiago got several rounds off at the Djinn. The first one hit, then he got his barrier back up and the next couple bounced away. An Elf screamed as one of the bullets found him.

Santiago's big Fae friend smashed down with his sword.

Somehow, the Djinn's shield held, although his forehead wrinkled with stress.

I took the moment to switch clips. Regular bullets didn't get through magical shields. I needed magic.

With a couple of tightly squeezed off shots, I covered his shield with lightning. The electricity danced over the shield. For a moment, the battlefield brightened like a sun had suddenly erupted in front of us.

It wasn't enough. His shield held.

The next time Vaern struck the shield, I fired again. It was a repeat of my first failed attempts. I hated the fact that even with my magical bullets, I couldn't get to him.

"If you're not going to use your claws, use the sword." Worf ran off to take down a pair of lizards that were rushing us.

He was right. He didn't know the sword had been crafted to take on Djinn.

Switching weapons, the raw power of the sword

surged through my arms. It was something I hadn't felt before. It was like it was responding to the Djinn.

I rushed him, for a second, it was like everything became a blur. Then Vaern and I smashed the shield together.

It flashed again, then went down.

The sudden disappearance in resistance left me falling forward. I rolled forward and came up in a crouch and lashed out at the Djinn.

A twin blast of power shot past me on either side. The Djinn dodged to the right, and the right one caught him and spun him around as my sword clipped him in the arm.

With a scream, the Djinn flew backward and turned to smoke. The dark cloud dissipated, vanishing from the battlefield before any of us could react.

Spinning around, I scanned the rolling hillside and couldn't see the smoke anywhere. The Djinn was gone, escaped before I could do more damage to him. The sword had damaged him. Urson's magic had performed as advertised. More than ever, I wanted to know more of what it could do.

"Lucas!" Harris shouted, then pointed his staff at the Dark Elves riding toward us. Lightning danced off the staff and struck one.

I followed his example and ran down the slope, sword held high.

22

I wasn't sure if it was Garnet's training or something about the magic in the sword, but I made smooth easy work of the Hun'se that came at us. They were skilled swordspeople, but I managed to counter every blow. The sword glowed with each blow.

A mage hurled a bolt of power at me.

Like the Orcs did with their shields and my bullets, I blocked with the sword. The magic flew off to the side, somehow hitting one of the lizards and dropping it in its tracks.

The queen's magic flashed over the field, bringing down lizards, and Elves alike. The Orcs weren't thrown to the ground unless they were knocked from their saddles. It appeared to be the same spell she'd used earlier but didn't seem to be as effective as it had been. More of the bad guys rose faster than they had before.

Our side bounced back like they'd just been gently knocked down. Vaern and the other giants didn't even stumble, and kept throwing their boulders, providing more and more obstacles on the green hills to slow the enemy advances.

The sword also protected me from the queen's

spell. I had fallen into the battle haze warriors did during a major fight. My wolf still lingered just under my skin, lending me his power as we hacked through Dark Elf armor, laying waste to them.

Santiago kept shooting as Worf slaughtered lizards and Orcs.

Vash's lightning cavorted across the battlefield, knocking Elves and Orcs to the ground. I'd never seen her throw so much power. It did seem like being in Faerie made her stronger.

I kept hacking away as Lum'se'el swarmed past me. They were more bloodthirsty than any people I'd seen before. The militants I'd fought in Afghanistan were always more than happy to kill Americans, but the Lum'se'el going after the Hun'se were downright ruthless. They weren't opposed to stabbing opponents in the back or running people through when they were struggling to stand. It was like a deep-rooted hatred drove their actions. When I'd been in the Rangers, we certainly were coldhearted killers, but we never let emotions cloud our actions. We were trained to turn off the emotions when we went into battle. The terrorists we fought against were just targets. Of course, they deserved what they got, but we were more clinical. The thing was, it was easy to be clinical from a warehouse roof, or the top of a sand dune hundreds of yards from the person you had in your sights. Fighting hand to hand or sword to sword was different. Maybe the other problem was the Lum'se'el and the Hun'se had been enemies for generations, and we'd only been at war with the Taliban for about twenty years. Generations were time to develop that deep hatred.

A Dark Elf came at me, and I managed to block his attack.

He pushed me back.

I swung high.

He blocked. His sword glowed as ours connected.

With all my strength, I slammed my sword down hard.

The blades slid across each other. Sparks blossomed as my sword edge clanged against his handguard. Bones cracked. He dropped the sword, shaking his hand.

Swinging the sword, I drove the point into his chest, ending him quickly.

Magic, bullets, and blades all cut through the air, sometimes drowning out the shouts and cries of the Elves dying around me.

A horn blared and instantly the Orcs turned and ran back down the hill. Seconds later, the Dark Elves followed.

The queen raised her sword and shouted, "Don't let them escape."

Around us, the Lum'se'el and their followers charged down the hill, continuing to attack the Hun'se.

Vash started after them.

I grabbed her arm. "Hold on. We don't do this."

She looked up. "Why, they're retreating?"

"She's got a point." Santiago paused and stooped down to pick up the sword my latest opponent had dropped. He studied the blade for a moment, then undid the belt that held the scabbard and strapped it around his waist.

"We fight differently." The last of the Fae had passed us, heading down the slope. Part of me wanted to say something about scavenging from the dead, but if all Santiago brought with him was his handgun, then he might be needing an additional weapon soon. As I was well aware, bullets didn't last forever.

"Are you guys coming, or just going to stand there staring off into nowhere?" Worf skidded to a stop and stared at us.

Santiago and Harris stared at me too.

"And he's got a point." Santiago gestured down the slope. "They're getting away."

I shook my head. "Retreating. There's a difference. I don't…" I paused. In the Rangers, we'd always pursued as far as we could.

"You don't feel right doing it." Harris finished for me. "I get it. These aren't our people. Let them handle their things and we can follow at our pace. We were already heading that way to go through the next barrier."

"Will we be disappointing the queen?" I watched as the Fae chased the others toward the barrier.

"Doesn't matter." Santiago rolled his neck. "I was hitching a ride with Vaern until the portals are opened again. I don't owe the queen anything."

Harris looked at me. "Do we owe her anything? Sure, we agreed to help, but if this turns into a slaughter, it's not cool. The thing is we don't know all the ins and outs of Elven politics."

"I think that's it." Something cold ran down my

spine. "What if they're running into an ambush?"

"What do you mean?" Harris stared after the fleeing armies.

I flashed back to the times in Afghanistan when terrorists had lured troops into ambushes. People often died. I didn't want that happening to the Lum'se'el.

"He means this could be a ploy." Santiago reloaded his gun. "Worf, you're the fastest of us. Get down there and watch their backs."

Over the next hill, even the giants had already disappeared. Their shouts had faded in the distance. Even the light show from the magic didn't illuminate the sky anymore.

"I can get us there too." Vash offered.

I glanced down. Even after the magic she'd been throwing around, her hair was still glowing as fiercely as it ever had. "It won't be too much?"

A thoughtful line crossed her smooth forehead. "Shouldn't be. It's not that far."

Worf had already taken off, running down the slope.

Santiago gave me a confused look. "What are you two on about?"

I grinned. There was a little bit of joy about knowing something about magic that someone else didn't.

Behind her, Harris put his hand on her shoulder.

As I took Vash's hand, I held out my other to Santiago. "Hold on."

Djinn magic engulfed us, but an ashy smell that wasn't Vash's hit me as we vanished. Something wasn't right.

23

I'd been through enough of Vash's teleports to not drop to the grass and vomit the way Santiago did. Turning loose of Vash's hand, I looked back up the hillside. "Effrit. Harris, we've got fucking Effrit up there."

Santiago wiped his mouth and stared at me. "What's an Effrit?"

"Dark Djinn." I pulled my sword and thought about running back up the hill toward them.

Before I could move, the first of the flaming skeletons came over the rise. They moved faster than anything human could've. There were six of them running in a tight formation. They arrowed toward us like some kind of silent, apocalyptic tide.

"Shit." Harris tensed as he took a step back from Vash.

"Was that big bad you had trouble with an Effrit?" Santiago stared, then glanced down at his gun. "Will bullets stop these guys?"

"Only if they're lucky ones." I pulled my sword. There were still stains on it from my fights. I felt a little bad about putting it up without wiping it down. Garnet would fuss for my oversight. "The catch is to hit them when they're solid."

"Solid?" Santiago pulled the sword he'd taken from the Dark Elf corpse.

"They're like Vash. Sometimes they're solid and sometimes they're smoke, ash, and flame."

Beside me, Vash gestured and a glimmering wall of power flared up between us and advancing Effrits. "I can't hold them long."

I didn't expect her to, especially against six Effrits. "Give us a chance." I glanced at Santiago. "Do you feel comfortable with the sword?" For a second I thought about handing Stormbringer to him, to give him an extra boost, but then remembered the spells Urson had laid on the weapon. It only worked for me.

He looked at the sword. "Do you know what makes this thing work?"

"Each one is different. You have to find out."

Harris pointed his staff and his power raged through Vash's protective shield. "No time. Use it and see what happens."

The Effrits hit Vash's defenses. She paled.

Worf showed up on the outside of the shield and hit the first one hard, bringing him to the ground.

Flames roared up around them. The stench of burning fur hit me as I dashed through the shield.

"Puppy!" Vash yelled and her power lashed out, crushing the flaming skeleton instantly into a pile of ash.

"Worf!" Santiago charged at my side and together we engaged the Effrits.

Glowing swords appeared in their boney grips. They blocked our blows with more skill than either of us had. Even with my months of training, they moved with years or more.

Once more, my wolf pressed himself tight against my skin. He granted me greater strength and speed, enough to match our magical opponent, but was it enough to make headway against him, especially when one of his friends joined him?

I blocked a blow coming at my head, then kicked at the second one.

The smell of burnt fur intensified as Worf knocked the second one down.

With a hard swing, I forced the remaining Effrit I fought back a step. It stumbled back a couple of steps and then Worf crashed into it at the same second that Vash's glowing force slammed into him. Between the two of them, he was crushed and his fires faded away, leaving only his battered skeleton beneath Worf's paws.

Turning, I rushed toward Santiago who was fighting two as well. Blood ran from a slash on his shoulder, but he was still swinging. His sword glowed with its own power. I wondered if it was from something he'd said or done, or if it was innate to the blade.

The Effrit I targeted turned to smoke as I slammed through it.

I stumbled at the lack of resistance.

It resolidified and brought his blade down toward my neck.

"No, you don't." Santiago blocked the blow, even as the other Effrit scored another hit on his arm. It was enough to save me.

Swinging hard, I came up under his arm. My blade came up almost on its own. It caught the Effrit hard in the side. Ribs cracked. Power surged through the blade. It glowed brighter than ever before. The Effrit screamed. Shrill, horrible sounds echoed through the air. It vacillated between solid and smoke. The smoke curled around the blade like some kind of snake. Slowly, at least it felt slow as time crept by, the screams faded, eclipsed by the sword's light. The brightness tore through the smoke, absorbing it and drawing it into the sword.

Magic blazed along the length of the blade and down the pommel. For a few seconds, it was like holding onto a live wire, then, along with the smoke, it died away. There was a greater weight to the sword, it wasn't much. How much does smoke weigh? But something had happened.

The remaining Effrit retreated out of our reach.

One of them blazed a little brighter than the others. "You can't entrap all of us. We are legion." He spun his hand around and all of them dissolved into their smoky form and vanished from the grassy battlefield.

I stared at my sword. Something had just happened, and I wanted to know what.

"We've got a bigger problem." Harris drew my attention away from the sword. He was pointing toward the glowing barrier at the realm's edge.

A hole already waited in the barrier, and just to the side of it, the dark-haired Djinn stood, a wide grin on his face as Orcs and Hun'se poured through the gap in the protection toward the Lum'se'el who were still pursuing the remains of the initial attack force down the slope. They outnumbered us. The queen was in trouble.

24

"Vash, can you close the opening in the barrier?" I glanced from her to the barrier. If we could cut off the flow of attackers, the Lum'se'el and their allies might have a chance to survive. The Dark Elves were trying to keep us from getting to their home turf.

Reinvigorated by their reinforcements, the attackers who'd been running from the queen's forces turned and renewed their assault. Several Orcs swarmed over one of the giant green plant warriors. I didn't think it was Santiago's friend Vaern, but I couldn't be sure. Sunlight glistened off axes as they swung frantically. Bark and sap flew as Harris, Santiago and Worf charged down the hill.

"I'll try." Vash got a focused look and pointed down the slope toward the barrier. Her power was a faint stream in the air as it connected with the point where the two realms came together.

The dark Djinn looked up toward us. A frown darkened his features and he stomped hard as the opening in the barrier began to shrink.

Vash moaned and wobbled for a moment, then she set her shoulders and more power flowed out of her.

Another source of power joined Vash's. I followed it back to the queen. A group of mages and warriors had surrounded her, protecting her from attack while she helped Vash attempt to close the opening in the barrier. If they could stop the flow of Dark Elves, we might be able to pull out a win.

Two Dark Elves charged us. I stepped between them and Vash, sheathing the sword and pulling Stormbringer. Targeting the closest one, I squeezed off a shot. I still had lightning bullets in the magazine. Thunder rolled across the battlefield and lighting arced as the bullet entered the Dark Elf. It exploded.

The second Elf dodged as I pointed the gun his direction. I followed him, anticipating his moves, and popped off another round. He jerked back away, avoiding the shot that exploded as it struck the ground a few feet away from him. He rolled as the electricity dealt him a glancing blow.

I got off another shot.

He blocked with his sword.

The round exploded, knocking the blade from his hand.

I shot again.

The Elf dodged the bullet.

He jumped toward me.

Somehow, I managed to land a punch. Even with my wolf augmentation, I was surprised I connected.

Stumbling, the Elf took a couple of steps back.

I pulled the sword.

As I slashed down, something stopped the blow. It was like I couldn't move the steel. Like it suddenly had a mind of its own.

The Elf slammed into me, knocking me down.

Dropping the sword, I grabbed him by the throat. Wolf wanted to bite, to crush his windpipe in powerful jaws, but I resisted. We had hands and thumbs, not fang and claws. With wolf's added strength, I twisted the Elf's head, snapping his neck. As a human would, he stopped moving, collapsing on top of me.

A grim satisfaction flowed from my wolf as he eased back just enough. There was a pleasure at discovering new ways to defend himself, ourselves.

I shoved the Elf off me and picked up the sword. There wasn't any resistance.

When I looked down toward the barrier, the opening had shrunk but was still open. Vash was on her knees, hands outstretched as she focused her power. Down, closer to the barrier, the queen still stood surrounded safely by her warriors and mages. The Djinn at the opening moved his hands in ever more complex motions, like he was trying to stay ahead of them, but failing.

An idea struck. He was distracted. He was a threat to Vash.

I pulled Stormbringer and carefully targeted. When I squeezed off the shot, the thunder that rolled out was louder, as if the gun and bullet both understood my need to take down the person I viewed as the biggest threat to Vash. He'd already kidnapped her once. I had to protect her.

Less than a second before the bullet would've struck, the Djinn went smoky. The bullet passed through him and hit the barrier. Lightning coursed across the magical wall. In a flash, the opening closed, cutting off the flow of Orcs and Hun'se. Shouts went up around the battlefield.

The Djinn resolidified and pointed at me.

His power struck, sending me flying head over heels up the slope. The hard landing forced the air out of my lungs. I gasped as my head swam.

"Lucas!" Vash screamed.

I had to get up. I had to protect her. The sword was the only thing that seemed to make the other Djinn slow down. I drew it again as I rolled back to my feet. Around me, the world shifted. The green hills convulsed like an earthquake had just struck.

Cacophony died away. It felt like I was being pulled out of the battle. Everything focused down. I couldn't see or hear anything. The sword was still in my hand. I tightened my grip. It was the only thing that felt real.

"Down." A deep voice rumbled through my mind. "Let me down."

Nobody was around. I glanced about. Even Vash was missing.

"Who are you?" I was alone. I felt like a man. There was none of my wolf's feral side. Something had cut off my connection.

"Turn me loose." The voice demanded. "I will *not* be controlled by the likes of you."

"What are you talking about?" The voice came from all around me. I needed something to focus on. I had to get back to the battle. Vash was in danger.

The sword grew warm in my hand.

"You have no right to hold me captive. Let me go." The sword shook as it got downright hot.

I flashed in my head that the voice was the spirit of the Effrit that I'd killed. Urson had said the sword could capture an Effrit, hold it prisoner, bind it to the sword like Vash was bound to her bell.

"No." I focused on the sword. "I defeated you, and you're mine to command." Words held magic. If there was anything I'd learned from the magic users around me, that was it. "You tell me to let you go. No. I will not let you go. You were trying to hurt Vash. Now and forever you will never hurt her again."

Dark smoke curled out of the sword. On the strange vacant landscape, an Effrit materialized. His glaring red eyes blazed into me. "You have to defeat me before you can control me."

I hadn't had to defeat Vash when she came out of the bell the first time. Had she been beaten down when she had first been bound to the bell? I didn't know, but I didn't have time to think about it.

The Effrit hit me hard. Knocking me back into the grass.

I rolled before he could land a kick on me.

The heat from his fire scorched me as I made it back to my feet. He grabbed at me.

Ignoring the flames licking off the bones, I slammed my shoulder into his rib cage. Bones cracked. I carried him down to the ground. For some reason, he didn't turn to smoke. I pounded him hard in the face.

His sharp cheekbones cut my knuckles. It was something else to ignore. I didn't have the wolf to draw on. It was like fighting an ambush terrorist who managed to get the first blow in and knock my rifle away. All I had was my fist and my wits.

The Effrit shoved me off. I rolled again, trying to get far enough away that I could get to my feet.

A short distance away, the sword lay in the grass. It glowed with a soft yellow light that was a sharp contrast to the Effrit's red flames.

I ran toward it. If the sword could contain the Effrit in the real world or even Faerie, maybe it could defeat him in the world I found myself. I ran and dove for the sword as the Effrit tried again to get his hands on me. Rolling more like a wolf than a man, I snatched the sword up and swung as I got to my feet.

As the sword passed through the flames to bounce off his spine, the Effrit screamed. I wanted to clamp my hands over my ears to block out the sound, but I swung again.

Raising an arm, the Effrit tried to block my next blow. The sword glowed brighter with each swing that connected and cleaved bone.

"No." The Effrit turned and ran up the hill. Its glow was diminishing with each second. There was barely a hint of a flaming corona around it dark brown bones.

I charged after him, swinging at the back of his neck. The sword connected. Smoke and cinders exploded outward as the Effrit's bones collapsed to the ground. Weaving the sword about in the smoke, I collected the Effrit's essence. Or maybe it was the sword that did.

"Ash." The name rang out loud and clear as the landscape faded away until I once again stood on the battlefield, back in time to block a Dark Elf attack that would've left me with a sword sticking out of my own ribcage.

Down by the barrier, the older Djinn glared up at me, there was pure hatred in his eyes as I stepped between him and Vash. The dominance fight with the sword didn't seem to take more than a couple of seconds, no matter that it had felt longer. I was still there, still capable of defending Vash, of keeping him from whatever prize she was for him.

25

Holding Ash high, I advanced toward the Djinn. Around me, the Light Fae and their allies battled with the Dark. None of them seemed to know me as I headed toward the Djinn whose name I didn't even know. I owed him for kidnapping Vash. He'd threatened her and me. He knew that to get control of her, he had to kill me.

Worf and Santiago were laying a swath of destruction through the Dark Elf ranks. The bad guys were still using swords, knives, and arrows. They weren't prepared to deal with bullets. Worf's claws and fangs weren't as dangerous, but he made up for that with his sharp mind.

The Djinn waited for me at the barrier. A dark nebula danced around him.

I kept Ash out. Its power rolled down its pommel and up my arm. The energy merged with my wolf. I growled.

A bolt of power came off the Djinn's outstretched hands.

Jerking Ash in its way, I sent the bolt off into the sky where hopefully it wouldn't hurt anyone. There wasn't even a jolt of pain from the impact. Ash took the energy like it was little more than a gentle breeze.

Unbidden, a sly grin crossed my face. I hadn't expected Ash to be able to do something like that. Had it always had that kind of power or was it something new, after I had killed the Effrit and Ash absorbed its spirit? What more could it do?

A ball of fire erupted from the Djinn's hands. It was a flaming comet heading toward me.

I took a wide stance, almost like a baseball player and turned Ash's flat side toward it, and swung right before the fireball would've hit me.

Again, the new power surged through me and when Ash met the fireball, I slammed the magic away. The fireball didn't deflect the same way the magical bolt did. It flew back toward the Djinn, but angled up and slammed into the barrier behind him.

He didn't send anything else toward me as I stalked toward him.

Power from the battlefield flowed around me. The Djinn seemed to be drawing it in, using the violence and death to make himself stronger. I wasn't sure what kind of creature could feed on death. When he held Vash, he'd staged his stand in one of the areas that had been most damaged in recent years. He was more dangerous than I'd realized. I just hoped Ash would give me the power to overcome.

With a frown, the Djinn conjured a sword covered in black flames.

I stopped stalking and charged, hoping to use a bit of momentum to my advantage.

Ash slashed through his defenses. The shield he quickly created shattered in a display of sparks that faded away the same way Vash's hair sparks did.

He brought the black flame sword up to block my attack. It held, but he stumbled back a single step.

The Djinn thrust back, rocking me on my heels. He slashed toward my head.

It was my turn to block. Ash absorbed the force of the blow, adding its power to his. The sword's glow increased.

"Fall, Wolf." The Djinn spat through gritted teeth.

"No." I punched toward his face.

He dodged backward and swung up his blade. It stuck Ash's narrow wrist guard and sent tingles through my arm.

As it slid along the wrist guard, the blade nicked my arm, even through the silver Elven mail. Pain seared through me. It invigorated me. My wolf, still close to my skin, snapped our teeth shut and then snarled. He took the burn as his own and helped me jerk away. I dropped to the ground and rolled back, under the Djinn's attack. I came up, just out of range, and braced myself for another round.

The Djinn pressed his attack and came at me.

I blocked the blow and Ash sent out a beam of light at the Djinn. He blocked, but the light caught him in the chin. Something about the light made him react worse than he had before. He shouted in a language I didn't know, and that Vash's translation spell didn't react to.

"I take it that hurt." I grinned again as I kept up the attack.

Slashing with all my strength, I hacked Ash

through his flaming black blade. The magic of the sword vaporized. The blow landed on the Djinn's shoulder. He shouted again as he turned to smoke. Like before, he faded from view.

"Come back here and fight like a man." I swung Ash through the smoke like I had when battling the Effrit. It didn't appear to have an effect. None of the smoke was drawn to Ash.

Magic light drew my attention. The queen and her mages were launching a last-ditch attack on the Hun'se. The fire they called lanced out into every crevasse and nook possible. Dark Elves and their allies went down. Orcs and giants fell to the burning ground. In the middle of the ring of mages and warriors, the queen's head dropped.

I glanced up toward Vash, where she stood a short distance from the bulk of the fighting. The red sparks from her hair fell to the ground in slightly diluted glows. She was tired. We all were. Santiago and I weren't used to the intense hand-to-hand fighting. I doubted Harris was used to fighting at all. Our downtime since leaving the World Tree had been minimal. I was ready for it to be over.

The remaining Lum'se'el warriors spread out through their burning opponents. I didn't agree, but I understood that they needed to be sure the Hun'se and their allies weren't going to be a problem. It made me wonder why Yas'Fe'el hadn't used the spell earlier. There was enough about magic I didn't know, maybe like getting a pot to boil it took time to build up to something so impressive.

"Lucas." Harris waved at me from the trunk of a tree he was leaning against.

"Harris, are you okay?" I slipped Ash back into his scabbard as I hurried over to him. The motion was still awkward with the mail.

Closing his eyes, he shook his head. A streak of blood dribbled down his forehead and to his cheek. "Not really. I always thought battle was supposed to be something people write ballads of. It doesn't feel like this is ballad-worthy."

"It's not." I did my best to not watch the Elves finish off foes who couldn't fight back. It was so much more visceral when we were in the middle of the battlefield than when we used modern weapons to take them out from a distance. "Do you need a healer?"

"I don't know." Harris shrugged. "My head hurts like hell."

"Okay, then. Let's get you some help." I waved at Vash to come down.

She vanished from the slope and appeared next to Harris. "Is it over?"

"For now." I looked her over. Other than slightly tired, she appeared to be okay. "Can you watch Harris while I go find a healer for him?"

"Sure." She took a couple of steps over to him and took his hand. "We'll be okay."

As I headed toward the queen's guards, I glanced around for Santiago and Worf. They were easy to spot. The big wolf next to him made Santiago stand out amongst the other warriors. I waved at them and then pointed toward the tree where Harris and Vash waited. Santiago raised his sword in acknowledgment as he headed their direction.

Slyl'fard broke away from the other Elves and walked toward me. "Thank you for aiding in the fight."

"Turns out it was more my fight than I realized." I stared at his battered armor. He'd obviously been deep in the fighting and hadn't taken time or power to magically clean up. Somehow, the lack of shiny made him so much more real.

"You took out the Djinn they have working with them." Slyl'fard grinned. "Not many of us have that kind of power."

"And that's probably a good thing." I was still learning about magic and power, but somehow the idea of Elves with more power was a little scary.

"Fahir Salabim is dangerous, to everyone standing against him." A dark look crossed his face. "That is one of the things we don't trust about those of mixed blood."

"Those like Vash." I didn't need him to glance in her direction to know what he was talking about. "I didn't know his name."

Slyl'fard gave the briefest of nod. "We've been monitoring his interactions with the Hun'se as close as possible for years. From what we know, he's unbound. That makes him even more dangerous." He pointed to my pocket where Vash's bell hid. "He's manipulating the Hun'se, but they don't trust us, so there's nothing we can do about it. You and your blade are the first time we've seen him defeated. We know he wasn't killed, but you gave us hope."

I wasn't used to giving people hope. Words failed me, so I defaulted to the reason I'd come down to the Elves in the first place. "Look. I need a healer. Harris has a head wound."

"The queen will take care of him. We appreciate what you've done." Slyl'fard turned and headed into the press of Elves.

For a moment, I stood there and studied them. There were so many similarities between them and the soldiers I was used to. They were tending to their wounded. Like Slyl'fard, the shiny veneer had come off and left them battered and bruised. I'd been in enough battles to know that once all the wounded were tended to, the partying would start. What I didn't know was if they would wait to get back to the world tree, or their home villages before they began their celebrations. We hadn't made it to the Hun'se citadel, but they were worn out and looked like they were ready to bail. If they had scored a heavy enough hit, then hopefully we had done enough for them to rethink hitting the Lum'se'el, at least for a while. What I didn't know was how long a while was for an Elf.

We had the name of the Djinn who was after Vash. I knew he was like her, a hybrid. But there were more questions. I knew what being bound meant, but I didn't know what being unbound did. If it made a Djinn more powerful, then Fahir Salabim was even more dangerous than we understood. Maybe, if I got really lucky, I could find someone who understood more about Djinn who could fill in the blanks. It was the blanks, so many blanks that were getting to me.

I turned back to the tree where I'd left my unit…my friends. As I walked back, the smell of burned flesh bore into my nose. I shook my head, but couldn't dislodge the scent. With a soft whine, my wolf retreated to the depths of my soul where he coiled and waited for the next time he was going to be needed. Vash was safe and that's what mattered most to both of us.

"You still okay?" I looked at Harris.

Sitting at the base of the tree, he had a cloth pressed to his cut. "Yeah. Vash made this cloth for me."

"I offered bandages too." Vash patted his shoulder.

"I figure we'll see what the healer does for me."

Santiago leaned on his staff. "Not sure I'm going to get used to the healers fixing every little thing."

"I don't think magic is supposed to be used for every little thing." I shook my head. "If we cure every little hurt with magic, we don't really live. Or at least that's what I've heard through the grapevine."

Yang'fard and the queen walked toward us.

"David Lucas, you are a mighty warrior." The queen smiled, but it wasn't enough to remove the dark circles under her eyes. "I admit that I had my doubts. Humans…werewolves aren't often the most stable or noble creatures. The Hun'se have been our dark cousins and our foes for more years than human memory. Rarely have we seen the fearlessness that you showed standing against our foes. Thanks to your valor, the Hun'se have sued for peace. It's a start."

I stared at her. Sure, I'd won medals and awards

of valor before. But somehow the words of the inhuman woman standing in front of me hit me hard. I swallowed. "I was defending my daughter."

Yas'Fe'el glanced past me, to the tree where Vash was with Harris. "Daughter? Wolves are often taking in strays." Her face softened. "Can you explain to her that we cannot acknowledge her? Not at this point. She has a great protector in you. Can I entrust you to continue to keep her safe?"

"Yes." I nodded. "I will always keep her safe. You don't need to ask."

"But I have. All you have to do is ask, and if it is within our power, we…my king and I, will provide." She glanced at the tree. "I need to go and help my people."

An Elf in blue silk robes covered in blood splashes approached. "My queen, I understand there are wounded here."

She waved toward the tree. "Yes, attend the human mage."

As he turned toward them, she smiled again. "David Lucas. The portal network will be open again soon. Your fight here is done. Go home. Hide Vash away from the other Djinn. Give her a good life."

I bowed to her. Rangers didn't bow to people, but I bowed.

Then she turned and walked back to her troops with Yang'fard at her side.

The healer had finished working on Harris by then and was walking back to the Fae who needed him more than we did. I returned to my unit, my family. It was time for us to go home. I could only hope the queen was right and the threat was dealt with, at least for a time.

26

Harris looked better when I got to the tree. The healer had done good work and there wasn't any blood running down his forehead, although he still looked pale and tired. I figured we all looked tired after the day we'd had.

"The queen says the portal network will be back up shortly." I squatted in front of Vash. "How are you feeling?"

"This place invigorates me." Vash smiled and looked smug. The diluted brightness of her normal orange and yellow sparks told me the truth.

"Hey," Santiago said from behind me. "Do you mind if I go find Vaern and make sure he's okay?" He sighed and shook his head. "Before yesterday, I wouldn't have thought about caring about a Fae."

"People can surprise us." I'd had plenty of surprises in recent months. "Changes happen, sometimes easier and more subversively than we expect. Go check on your friend. We need to find out where a portal is that we can use to get back to Earth. That might take some time. Go make sure he's okay."

"Thanks, Lucas." Santiago gave the briefest of nods, then glanced at Worf. "Come on, let's go so we can get back."

"Sure, Theo." Worf fell in beside him and the two of them headed off toward where some of the giants who'd fought alongside the Lum'se'el had gathered.

I sat next to Harris.

Vash plopped down in front of us.

"I have a name." I sighed. "The name of the Djinn. Is there anything we can do with it?"

Harris rubbed his chin. "Names have power, a lot of it. I need my books, and maybe books from some of our friends. There're some things we can do. Might be able to find a way to dilute his power when he attacks. There might even be some way to create a cloaking spell that would hide Vash from him."

"Then yeah, we need to get back to Earth and dig up the info. We have to stop Fa-"

Putting his finger on my lips, Harris shook his head. "Don't say it. There might be some chance he'll be listening, particularly here in a realm just one adjacent to the home of his Fae allies."

"Names have power," I repeated. I wanted to learn so much about magic so I wouldn't make stupid mistakes like saying the name of a creature that might be able to hear me and be drawn to me and Vash. The more I knew, the better I could do that job the queen had given me.

"Right." Harris patted my cheek. "I still say Garnet's going to be mad that she missed out on this."

I laughed.

Vash giggled. "Yeah, she is."

"So, once Theo comes back, we'll still need a Fae to help us find a portal." Harris folded up the cloth he'd been holding to his forehead.

Pointing at the cloth, Vash smiled. "Do you need that anymore?"

"No." Harris shook his head. "I think I'm done."

"Okay." Vash waved her hand and the cloth disappeared in the shower of blue sparks. "It wouldn't have lasted long anyway." She pursed her lips and looked a little serious. "I think I can create the portal to take us home."

"Do you have enough power for that?" I didn't like sounding as if I doubted her. She needed support. But I didn't want her to overextend herself. The level of her exhaustion still showed in her sparks. If she pushed herself too far, she'd fade away to her bell. It wasn't horrible, but I wanted her to have a normal life, and a normal life wasn't fading away and being bound to an inanimate object.

She jumped up and laughed. "I'm sure. Like I said earlier, this place juices me up."

I cocked my head. "Juices you up? Where did you hear that?"

"Garnet says it sometimes. Did I use it wrong?" A line of confusion crossed her forehead.

Harris laughed. "No. Sounds like you used it right."

"I just wasn't expecting you to say something like that." I joined in the laugh. It felt good. The high stress of the battle began to fade, although I didn't want to relax too much, we weren't' home yet.

Santiago and Worf returned with their friend

Vaern shaking the ground with each step he took.

"Vaern's offered to help us get to a portal to Earth." Santiago patted the big green guy's leg. "Says it might take a couple of portals to get to one."

Vaern smiled, his teeth looked more like thick bark than shiny enamel. "It's going to take a while, but hopefully the way will be safer than before. The Hun'se won't be stirring up trouble for a while."

The idea of it taking a while didn't make me happy. "Vash has suggested that she might be able to create a gate to get us home."

Vaern looked over at Vash. "A Djinn doesn't have the same limits as the Fae. Their power might be able to open a gate without it being anchored the way Fae gates have to be."

Again, there were things I didn't totally understand. When I stopped and thought about the gates we'd used on the way to the World Tree, they'd been in trees, on rock walls, inside the holes, and built into arches crafted in a circle. Each one had a permanence to it. They were really part of a network, like the magical version of an interstate system.

"I've never done it before, but I helped Harris activate the one back on Earth." Vash stood and paced a bit. "After going through the ones here in Faerie, I think I understand how the energies work. I should be able to make a portal home, back to the one we went through near the Sprite attack."

It made sense to me, like watching a man dance or fight to understand the steps and maneuvers. There were a lot of things we could learn by watching. She was an observant kid, fast to learn things when she saw them. I'd seen it in action, as she adapted to life in the twenty-first century.

"I think you can do it. Would it be better to wait until you're back to full strength?" I tousled her hair.

She stuck out her lower lip and looked a bit pouty. It was another thing she'd learned from some of the women around us. "I can do this. If everyone is ready."

I glanced at Harris, Santiago, and Worf. "We ready, guys?"

Santiago nodded. "I was ready when I got here." He looked up at Vaern. "See you around, big guy."

"Goodbye, Theo." Vaern hiked about halfway between us and the body of the Elven army before he turned and sat down, watching what was about to happen.

"You don't have to do this before we rest." I offered Vash another out to recharge.

She shook her head, sending red sparks dancing around her. "Let's do this." She sounded just like Cin Kilkari.

"Okay." Harris stood, and leaned on his staff just inches behind her. "I'm here if you need me."

"We all are." I motioned for Santiago and Worf to close ranks. Maybe if she didn't have to make the portal overly large, it might be easier for her.

"Thanks." Vash grinned over her shoulder, then started waving her hands as the sparks from her hair exploded in a brilliant display of magic. She flexed her hands back and forth as verdant energy danced from her fingertips to the air a couple of feet in front of her. The green energy slowly expanded from a small spot to a glowing portal large enough for any of us to walk through without having to stoop.

She wobbled a bit as she stopped moving her hands. "Okay. I think I got it. Energy's the same, but we need to move."

"Okay." I took her hand. "Let's get going." I wanted to get home, back to something I understood without questions.

Harris put his hand on my shoulder. "It might be easier if we're all touching."

"Sounds good." I kept hold of Vash as she walked into the portal's swirling light.

I lifted my foot to step into the portal, and a bony hand grabbed my foot. The green energy of the gate turned an angry red. Heat seared through me.

Vash screamed and we all tumbled through the portal.

Hot wind slammed into me, assuring me we weren't in the Colorado foothills.

The portal snapped shut behind us, and an Effrit lay on the beige sand, still clinging to my ankle.

Reflexively, I kicked it as hard as I could.

27

As the Effrit rolled away from me, I kicked it again.

Harris smashed its head with his staff. The blow didn't do much, not even a crack in its flaming skull.

"What the hell?" Santiago fired his pistol several times into the Effrit.

Worf bit into its leg and yanked it hard enough to pull the bones free of the Effrit's body. "Sword, Theo. Use magic." He spit out the femur and went for the other side.

Santiago pulled the sword he'd taken from the fallen Dark Elf and slashed down on the Effrit's hip girdle.

The Effrit screamed.

I scooped Vash up in my arms and backed off to give them room to finish the Effrit.

Her body was limp in my arms. She hadn't changed to smoke and retreated to her bell, but she was still.

My heart pounded. "Vash. Are you okay?"

She wasn't moving.

I felt for a pulse, then realized that I didn't know if Djinns even had a pulse. Something was wrong. Under my fingers, the faintest of pulses pounded. She was alive.

"Harris, something's wrong!"

The Effrit screamed again, then the sounds of struggle faded behind me.

"Lucas, what do you mean something is wrong?" Harris huffed as he came up and looked over my shoulder. "She should be in her bell when she's unconscious."

"That's what I thought." I cradled Vash's still form. She was heavier than I remembered, like she was more solid than ever before. "What's going on? What did the Effrit do to us?"

"Multiple questions." Harris gestured to the sand. "Lay Vash down, then we can see what we can sort out."

Glancing over at the unmoving, unglowing bones that had just been an Effrit intent on our destruction, I settled on the sand, and laid Vash in my lap. She moaned slightly, and I worried that I might have hurt her.

"First, I think Vash is just overextended, unless the Effrit somehow did something beyond assuming control of the portal." Harris knelt in front of us and brushed a hair off Vash's forehead. It looked like simple, normal red hair. No sparks fell to the sand. She appeared to be a normal, tired little girl. "We won't know that until she wakes up and can tell us what happened from her perspective."

"As to what it did to us? Well, we're not in Colorado. These aren't the Great Sand Dunes National Park."

"Looks like Afghanistan." I glanced up, feeling like we were back where all my changes had begun.

Worf sat just to my side. "We're not on Earth. Or at least not an Earth that I know. It's too clean. No smells of industry."

I frowned and took a deep breath. He was right. The odor of the sulfur that accompanied the Effrit was clearing. It was the cleanest air I'd ever smelled. Even though I was still adjusting to my enhanced senses, I knew the air was wrong, and wrong put all of us in danger.

What will it take to awaken Vash? Lucas and company search to find answers and their way home when their story continues in "Blaze" coming soon.

Other Books by A.M. Burns

Shifter Force
1: Visions of Rage
2: Visions of Shadows
3: Visions of Stars

Yellow Sky Coven:
1: Blood Moon Yellow Sky
2: Dark Stars of Dallas

Stand Alone Books:
The Black Fin Case

YA Books:
Coyote's Pup

Familiar Series:
1: Familiar Path
2: Familiar Spirit

Books in the Infragilis Universe.

Smoke and Moonlight
1:Spark

Solstice Properties Mysteries
1: Second Story Hex
2: Watchtower WooWoo
3: Mid-Century Monster

Tempest Academy Prologue
Running in a Pack
Into the Sky
Shifting Tides

Want to see the story behind Cin Kilkari's first encounter with Agent Briar and learn more about what life is like raising two witch daughters and dealing with the ghost of her mother, Be sure to check out the Solstice Properties Mysteries.

The Stone place.

It started out as just another house to renovate for Cin and Chad Kilkari. Of course, the skeletons in the backyard were just the start of major complications.

Magic and house flipping collide. Can the duo fix the house and save Cottonwood, Colorado from the dark magic buried there?

If you like snarky witches and charming werewolves, with a Southwest flavor, you can't miss this new cozy series. It's sure to keep you up all night until the last page that leaves you thirsting for more.

Don't wait, buy Second Story Hex today!

Available at your favorite bookseller.

Other Books by A.M. Burns

Blood runs deep in Jemez Springs.

Psychic cougar shifter Connor McGriffin is used to his visions leading him around. For years, he's followed them back and forth across the country to the people who need his help. When his comfortable vacation in the mountains is interrupted by a vision of a woman dying, he can't see enough details to find the killer and stop him from striking again. Facing the most dangerous foe he's ever dealt with, Connor needs all the help he can get.

Small town deputy and wolf shifter, Danny Lupan is getting bored of chasing speeders and the occasional drug dealer. When the call comes that Sandoval County has its first murder in years, and it happened in his jurisdiction, he jumps at the chance to find the killer, no matter the danger involved. Little does he know, he might lose his heart, his life, or maybe both.

When a cougar and a wolf join forces, the bad guys better watch out, because the fur's going to fly, in more ways than one.

Join Connor and Danny on their first adventure together in the start of the fast-paced, suspenseful thriller series Shifter Force.

Available at your favorite bookseller.

Blood Moon
Yellow Sky
Yellow Sky Coven Book 1
A.M. Burns

A war is about to break out, and the combatants are who everyone expects. Can a dragon and a young mage stand in the middle of it and hope to get out alive?

Tal O'Duirwood, druid dragon, enjoys his quiet life of solitude in the Colorado mountains. When the need arises, Tal is the one the Coalition of Magical Creatures calls on to handle problems no one else can. For years he's worked on his reputation as the thing of nightmares for those who step out of the shadows. He never realized what was missing from his life until his gets an assignment to travel to Yellow Sky, Texas and help a witch and her students there stop a vampire invasion. Once there, he finds things were not as he was told. The witch is actually a werecoyote, and one of her students has eyes for Tal. Can Tal help stop the vampires in time to save his blossoming love? Will his heart, so long closed off from the world, be able to open to the touch of the handsome young mage

Available at your favorite bookseller.

The
Black
Fin
Case
A.T. Weaver
&
A.M. Burns

For several months, Detective Greg Williams and his partner have been trying to catch the Black Fin gang. Their latest intelligence is good, so they go on their most risky raid yet. But things go horribly wrong. While recuperating from the wounds he received during the botched raid, Detective Williams and his captain realize there might be a leak in the Portland police department. When they begin digging, things get worse for Williams.

At the urging of his captain, Detective Williams heads into the mountains, hoping a little distance from the department will give the Black Fins and their police informants the opportunity to slip up. His working vacation soon takes turns he could never have imagined when he meets the reclusive writer, Ken Draiag, next door, who turns out to be more than Greg ever imagined. But the Black Fins aren't about to let Detective Williams rest, they soon track him down, but with Ken's help, Greg manages to stay alive and fight back as forces he never knew existed reveal themselves to be working against him. Will Greg survive the Black Fins' ultimate plot?

Available at your favorite bookseller.